Spooky Tells

Spooky Tells

Tanis Rush

Oak Tree Press  Hanford, CA

Oak Tree Press
Publishers Since 1998

SPOOKY TELLS, Copyright 2014, by Tammy Rushing. All rights reserved. Printed in the United States of America. No part of this book may be used or reproduced in any manner whatsoever without written permission except in the case of brief quotations used in critical articles and reviews. For information, address Oak Tree Press, 1820 W. Lacey Boulevard, Suite 220, Hanford, CA 93230.

Oak Tree Press books may be purchased for educational, business, or sales promotional purposes. Contact Publisher for quantity discounts.

First Edition, April 2014

ISBN 978-1-61009-120-6

LCCN 2012934517

This book is for my mother, Donnie Gail. She is my biggest fan.

Acknowledgements

I would like to thank authors Kay Hooper and Catherine Coulter for their imagination and wonderful stories which have been a great influence on my writing.

Chapter One

Detective Michael Balcher sat patiently in the dark shadows of his vehicle. From where he was parked, he could see his target's car and the entrance she'd just used to slip unobtrusively into the headquarters office building of Radicom Industries. This was the fourth night he'd watched her, but only the first night that she'd actually left her house in the evening. His surveillance of her was not work mandated, although he was a detective with the Las Vegas Police Department. No, this was an entirely personal errand. He had become nearly obsessed with finding out answers to this particular puzzle and he was at the point that he couldn't wait any longer to act on that obsession.

He checked his watch. It was after midnight. He slid down in the seat, just in case his considerable bulk was distinguishable in the lighted parking lot. She might be a while and he decided that he may as well make himself comfortable.

*   *   *

The thief was going for it.
Sarah 'Spooky' Knight put her camera closer to the glass partition and snapped another shot. The infrared film that had cost her a small

fortune was catching every damnable move the thief made in the near pitch darkness of the corporate president's office.

Yeah, that's it, slick. Take the bait. Come to Mama. Just a few more shots and it's sayonara, sucker.

She clicked away as he took several documents from the safe. Suddenly, his head jerked around to look her way.

She pulled out of sight into the gray darkness of the outer office, sliding the expensive camera into her canvas backpack and tossing it over her shoulder. She glanced around to gauge the distance to the hall and then to the elevator.

Not good! He'd see her if she made a run for it. Looking around, she spotted a large potted palm in a nearby corner; its fronds casting scarcely discernable dark shadows against the wall in the air conditioned emptiness of the office. She headed for the palm, barely having time to settle down behind it before he entered the room.

He eased into the outer office, his steps silent as he passed her and went to the hallway door to look out. He stood in the doorway rigidly for a few moments, his silhouette like a black hole surrounded by the dim glimmer of the emergency lights from down the hall. She could barely hear him breathe as he listened to the silence around him searching for whatever it was that alerted him to her presence in the first place. He turned in her direction and she saw the tiniest glint of something in his hand. Knife maybe? Or a gun?

She swallowed. Oh, please! Not again. She hated this. Frustrated, she carefully removed her camera from her backpack and concealed it in the dirt at the base of the potted palm. She had no choice; she could not take it with her.

"I can hear you," he said, his deep voice resonating in the darkness as he slowly stepped towards her, his body effectively blocking her exit.

She tensed as she got ready. This was going to hurt like hell.

Outta here!

She screamed those words inside her head and lights flashed through her mind, glowing with all the colors of the rainbow and then began to swirl together into a tornado that slammed through every cell of her body. Then she was gone.

The man eased toward the palm, its fronds swaying slightly as if blown by a gentle breeze. He waited until he was three feet away from it before he pounced. He knocked the plant over with one blow of his hand scattering dirt and plant matter in all directions. What he saw when everything settled stunned him.

There was nothing behind the palm but a pile of clothes and a backpack.

He whirled around, hairs standing at the base of his neck, knowing damned well that the intruder had been in the room. He saw no one. His foot hit something—a camera. He bent over and picked it up, his senses clanging. Chills skittered down his spine causing him to swear silently as he bolted for the elevator.

Balcher heard a car start up. He raised his head imperceptibly to look. The sound came from the other side of the building. He saw a flash of the headlights before the car pulled into the street and merged with traffic. Las Vegas was a 24/7 town, and traffic at two o'clock in the morning was not much different than two in the afternoon.

He glanced toward Spooky's car. It was still there, but something felt funny to him now. A few minutes ago he'd sensed her presence—the usual hairs on the back of his neck raised like antennae at her nearness—but now they were calm.

She could have left in that vehicle a few moments ago, but he didn't think so. Spooky was a loner, and in that, she was like him. He'd bet his last paycheck that she wouldn't have met someone here in the middle of the night. Still, he had the disturbing impression that he could wait here, watching the building all night, and it wouldn't matter.

Determined, he settled in to wait, anyway.

* * *

"*Arrrgggghhhhhh!*" Spooky screamed the unintelligible epitaph as she materialized inside her bedroom in her apartment. The sound spewed helplessly from her mouth as her feet hit the floor. She stumbled, barely getting her balance before the pain bent her over double, her naked body trembling from the intensity of it.

She slid to the floor and waited for it to stop. It never lasted for more than a few seconds and this time was no exception.

When the pain eased up, she was sweating profusely. Sucking in harsh breaths, and feeling ten times weaker than a wrung out dishrag, she crawled to her bed and got under the covers in anticipation of the second reaction to her 'trip'. The massive metabolic spike that fueled her 'trips' always left her chilled to the bone.

She felt the cold wash over her as if she had been dunked in the ocean at the peak of winter. As bad as that first bolt of pain was, this was worse. It sure as hell didn't abate as fast. Her body began shaking uncontrollably and her teeth chattered. She pulled the covers up under her chin and wished heartily for a hot bath. If she had the strength to crawl to the bathroom, she would have gone that route. She pulled her legs up to her chest, hoping skin against skin would hurry the process, but knowing it wouldn't.

Think about something else!

As usual, her mind marveled over the fact that all of this was possible in the first place. She had studied biology extensively at college a few years back and what she learned there only confirmed a few of her own conclusions. This talent of hers—there was no other word for it—had nothing whatsoever to do with magic. It was pure biology. The kind of metabolism it took for her to 'trip' was analogous to a hot burning furnace. She burned calories at a massive rate. To compensate, she had formed a habit early in life of eating at least five thousand calories a day just to keep the ol' furnace stoked. It wasn't difficult. She was always starving.

People smiled at her in restaurants, amazed at the amount of food she consumed. She was so thin, they probably thought she was anorexic or maybe the victim of an ogre of a husband or boyfriend who kept her half-starved all the time. She didn't care what they thought. She didn't care what anyone thought. She got over that years ago.

She was a highly sought after private detective now, no longer the skinny geek of a teenager that had been bounced from one foster home to another and from one town to the next. It took a quirk of fate, but she eventually found her niche, her purpose in life, an awesome way to use her gifts and make a living at the same time.

Her chattering teeth slowed imperceptibly. Sometimes it comforted her to think back to the day her luck began to change. It was one of the few good memories she had. She'd been hauled into the Las Vegas police station after she witnessed a mugging. The police station was the last place she would have gone voluntarily had she been asked, which, of course, she hadn't. Lingering shame from her childhood—and her less than law abiding mother who had landed in jail for ten years when she was barely six years old—had her hoping to fade into the woodwork as she waited with the other riff-raff who were at the station for God only knows what reasons.

The station was busy and overly loud, reminiscent of the inside of a casino, which was appropriate for Las Vegas. While she waited, a man brushed against her and she 'flashed' on something.

His daughter was missing.

And she knew who had her, or at least some information that would lead to the man who had her.

That was her other unique talent—something people from the paranormal world called being a touch telepath or clairvoyant. She could see things, flashes, images like a video reel at the brush of a hand or sometimes by touching something that belonged to a person.

Although she hated the derision she faced every time she admitted to being a psychic, she wasn't comfortable keeping what she had just seen to herself. The horrible man who had taken the little girl was going to kill her, if he hadn't already. Her visions were not always clear. Sometimes she saw things that had already happened, some even years ago. Most, though, were in the present. Very few of them had been of the future. She could count those on one hand and have fingers left over.

That day, she had not been exactly sure of what she had seen, but she was reasonably sure it was in the present. She went to the front desk and asked the desk sergeant for the name of the man in charge of the precinct. He tried routing her through the proper chain of command, but she was able to get the information she wanted by touching his desk.

It happened that way sometimes. She could ask a question and then touch something that the person she was questioning was touching and she would get a glimpse of what they were thinking. Not in words, exactly, but in images that she could put together to form a conclusion. In this case, she saw the path through the building that ended at an office with the name Davenport lettered in gold on the glass door.

She marched back to the head man's office, knocked once, entered and found herself in the presence of the best looking male she had ever seen in her life. Although immediately bumfuzzled, she blurted out that she was psychic and explained what she had just seen in her head, right down to a description of the man in her vision who had a small scar under his left eye and a chipped front tooth. Better yet, she'd seen the make and color of his car, and his license plate. It was all part of her vision when she saw him push the crying girl into his trunk and shut it.

She waited for the inevitable derision she endured each and every time she tried to convince someone that she was psychic. It did not happen. The man she later came to know as Captain Jim Davenport appeared to take her information seriously, even to the point of asking her for more details of her vision. He wrote down everything she said and made a few calls. Then he took her name and asked if she would sit with a police artist for a sketch. She did.

She found out later that he had been playing her. He had originally thought that she was in on the abduction, but for some reason, chickened out and made up the psychic story to justify her information. It took some fast talking and a few parlor tricks to convince him otherwise. She touched his briefcase and got a vision of a stock going bad—he must have kept his stock portfolio in there, which seemed to her to be strange behavior for a police captain. But come to think about it, he did look more like a Wall Street executive than a cop. She told him about the stock price falling drastically and then waited patiently for him to call his stockbroker to check out her story. His frown when he hung up confirmed her vision was accurate, which was not always the case. Not that her visions weren't usually good, she just didn't always interpret them correctly.

That incident started a strange and unsatisfying relationship between her and Captain Jim. Unsatisfying, because he never seemed to notice that she was female—which, for the first time in her life was unusually important to her—and strange, because friends were something other people always had, never her. Not to mention that every time she entered the LVPD to see Captain Jim, she inevitably encountered her nemesis, Detective Michael Balcher. That man was a bulldog and she was apparently a bone that he could not resist.

Just being in the same building with him made the hairs on the back of her neck stand up. She'd never before been able to sense anyone's presence like she could Balcher's. At first, she thought it was

Davenport causing this reaction, but after a while she realized that the sensation intensified every time she came within shouting distance of Balcher. She didn't know what it meant, but she eventually came to the conclusion that he was somehow dangerous to her. Not that he would physically hurt her. She didn't sense that. It was just a weird feeling that getting too close to him would end her existence as she knew it.

And she had the strangest feeling that he could sense her the same way. She often saw him rubbing the back of his neck and looking at her strangely. Maybe that's why he was so often sarcastic with her. It might be some kind of self-defense mechanism.

She snuggled deeper under the covers and decided to banish all thoughts of Balcher. They were not conducive to her happiness. She preferred thinking about Captain Jim. At lease he was pleasant to her, and she felt she owed him for his confidence in her. After their first successful collaboration, he found many uses for her, all of them unofficial and discrete, missing persons cases mostly, although he did pester her for a stock tip once in a while. The stock thing she could not help him with. She would have had to see the future for that and those instances were rare and always had something to do with an event of importance. Her success rate with the missing persons cases, however, prompted a joke from him that she would make a decent private detective. The idea stuck. When he saw she was serious, he helped her to get her P.I. license.

She started out with missing persons cases, of course, but eventually she got other work. The casinos loved her. She'd routed out more card counters in one year than they'd caught in the last ten years using more conventional investigators. And then, there were the more sophisticated investigations like tonight's case where she was in the process of catching an industrial spy.

The money she made catching card counters for the casinos was amazing and there was definitely less heartbreak working those kinds of jobs than there was working missing persons cases. Most of the time, missing persons cases turned bad fast. She'd found more graves over the last three years than she cared to count. She had also found people who did not want to be found; they had left home of their own volition and had no intention of coming back to loved ones that missed them terribly. There have been wives or husbands who have run away with lovers, leaving their children and spouses heartbroken. Missing persons cases that ended well were few, but they made the rest of them palatable.

Her shivering was beginning to lessen. She rolled over in bed to warm her other side. This was not exactly the way she had planned to spend this night. She should have been celebrating the successful end of her case. Instead, she was going to have to start all over if she could not retrieve her camera.

"Dammit!" she growled under her breath as she thumped her pillow hard. She hadn't done any tripping for more than a year now. It had always, *always,* been her last resort. No one in their right mind would go through the pain tripping caused just for the hell of it.

The dread she eventually experienced every time this happened came slithering into the back of her mind. The mysterious process of tearing herself apart and putting herself back together was surely harming her in some infinitesimal way. That was the main reason she only tripped during emergencies. Counting tonight, in all her twenty-six years she has only tripped eleven times. Since she was not a quantum physicist, she could not explain what happened to her as she went flying through the air in the form of pure energy. She only knew that when the trip ended, she was usually five pounds or so lighter and mostly useless for the next week as she exhibited symptoms of flu with all the chills and body aches normally associated with that sickness.

She felt her stomach begin to gnaw on her backbone and weakly reached to the nightstand drawer for the cookies she kept there. She munched on them as she wondered about the man she left back in the Radicom offices tonight. The camera lens was set for night vision, so she got a fairly good, if color distorted, look at him. He was not one of Radicom's employees as she originally thought.

She felt a glimmer of premonition, mostly just a *really* bad feeling about this case. It worried her. The intruder struck her as having a hardness within him, his emotional aura one of relentlessness. Probably just her imagination. She found herself praying that the camera and the evidence it contained was safe. She would feel better with this man in jail where he could not get to her. She shivered, and this time it was from a deep seated fear. Tonight changed things; she could feel it in the air, smell it. The world around her had changed perceptively, the colors, lines, and shapes were sharper, more defined, dangerous. She tried to shake off the uneasiness. It was probably the trip that had her mind playing tricks on her.

That and the uneasy thought that this time she might not have put herself back together correctly.

Chapter Two

That incessant ringing was nearly driving her crazy. She jerked awake and the dream of a phantom phone ringing in the clouds spilled over into reality. She grabbed for the phone, nearly knocking it off the nightstand. "Spooky Knight," she growled into the handset.

"Wake up, Sunshine," a pleasant voice said over the phone.

"Jim? What time is it?" she asked grumpily.

"Nine o'clock. Get your skinny butt out of bed and get down to the station. I need you."

"Now?" she asked, her speech still slurred from sleep. "Can't it wait? I'm sick," she said, a bit of pleasure seeping in as she realized that he had noticed her butt, whether he thought it was skinny or not.

"Nope," he said. "And don't grumble. I've got a witness here and—"

"You want me to be your lie detector again," she finished for him, dragging herself into a sitting position and letting the bed covers fall to her waist. Her bedroom was sweltering, a vast difference from last night.

"Fifteen minutes," he said and hung up before she could answer.

"Great," she muttered at the empty dial tone sounding in her ear. She hit speed dial three and got her favorite cab company on the line. After making arrangements for a ride, she slammed the phone down on the bedside table before jumping out of bed.

Actually, it was more like falling out of bed. Her knees wobbled as she went to the dresser to find a pair of jeans and a t-shirt. What she saw in the mirror actually startled her. This was her all time worst look ever. Her hair would have made Phyllis Diller proud and her face was gaunt as a skeleton. "Freakin' great," she mumbled.

She ran her bony fingers through the tangles of her dark brown curly hair in an effort to calm the bush into something a little less frightening and then she went into the bathroom to brush her teeth. After that, she weighed in. One hundred and five pounds. Seven pounds less than yesterday. Her shoulders fell in disgust. Pulling on her clothes, she went to the full length mirror—a mirror that she obviously put on the bathroom wall as some kind of self-castigating torture device—and looked over her five foot, eight-inch frame. She *was* a skeleton. Her jeans were barely hanging onto her bony hips.

She looked at her chest and frowned. "Never fear, Wonder Bra is here," she muttered as she went back to her dresser and ransacked her underwear drawer. At least, she would have the illusion of breasts, although why she bothered was a mystery. Jim never looked at her as a woman. Well, maybe if every other female on the planet suddenly disappeared, he would. But until such a mass exodus occurred, she needed to get that idea right out of her head.

Jim accepted her as a psychic, and he might even be able to wrap his mind around the idea of teleportation if she ever got the courage to bring it up to him, but the debonair Captain Jim could have any woman he wanted. And he liked them beautiful if the steady flow of female flesh she saw coming and going over the years was anything to go by. Spooky would be as welcome to his collection of women as a clump of ragweed would be to a bouquet of exotic flowers.

She pulled her boisterous long hair into a ponytail and decided, like every other day of her life, not to bother with makeup. She grabbed a duplicate set of her keys and headed out the door to wait on the cab.

The traffic in downtown Las Vegas was gnarly, but the cabbie was doing better navigating his way to the Radicom building than she would have done. He left her at her car and she glanced at the clock on the dashboard as she cranked up. Davenport's order to be there in fifteen minutes was a joke—unless she teleported, she thought. It was not a serious thought. Doing it again so soon would kill her. Besides, she could not trip just because she was late for an appointment. It would not 'do' to show up for a meeting naked.

She had never been able to bring clothes or any other inanimate objects with her on one of her trips. She was not sure why. She never consciously decided to do it one way or the other. Maybe deep inside her strange mind, she was afraid that she would not reconstitute herself correctly if she tried to bring anything with her. She could just imagine herself with cloth woven into her skin or a zipper lining her spine or worse. She had nightmares about it occasionally, especially after she read Dean Koontz's novel, *The Bad Place*. She must have read that book a hundred times after it came out. She tried to contact the author several times but he never responded to any of her letters. It did not matter. He probably thought she was a nutcase.

She pulled into the parking lot of the LVPD and went in. Officer Hamrick at the desk motioned for her to go on back. They all knew her here as a personal friend of the captain's. They didn't know why she was allowed such casual access to their leader, but they never questioned it. Well, most of them didn't, she thought as she ducked around the corner to keep from running into Detective Michael Balcher. The hairs on her neck told her he was close by.

Too late. He saw her.

"Well, well, look what the cat dragged in," he drawled with his particular brand of sarcasm. "You look like you've been rode hard and put up wet." His left eyebrow rose as he looked her up and down.

"Who asked you?" she asked, trying to get around his considerable bulk. The man was lumberjack huge, as big as that Brawny guy on those paper towel commercials. He wore his nearly black hair in a crew cut and looked like he'd just stepped off of a Marine Corps recruitment poster. He was about six foot, five inches tall and two hundred and sixty pounds, if she had to guess. He had intense, dark brown eyes that missed nothing. Even with all that, he was sort of attractive. That is, if you liked the commando type.

"Nobody, Spookaaayyyy," he said, saying her name the way he knew she hated it to be said. "How'd you get that name anyway?

Must have scared the doctor when you popped out."

"It's a nickname," she answered as she eased her way around him and headed for Jim's office. She learned a long time ago that it was best not to get into it with Balcher. Something about her set the man off, big time. Most of the guys at the station got along with him fine, so it was probably just her ugly face that set his teeth on edge.

He followed her. "Nickname, huh? What'd you do to make someone call you Spooky?"

"It was a Halloween prank that stuck, that's all," she said, giving out her standard response. There was no need to tell him about the time she accidentally touched a class mate at school and blurted out things about him that no one had any business knowing. After that, even the teachers were careful around her. Half-way through first grade she was the most shunned kid at school and indelibly stuck with the nickname Spooky.

That year taught her just how different she was from everybody else. She learned not to touch anyone if she could help it, but if she did, not to say anything she learned through that touch. So began a life of isolation that she was still living.

"He'll never be interested in you, you know."

"Who?" she asked, uncomfortable with the memories of her childhood and even more uncomfortable with Balcher as he followed her way too close. He looked almost as tired as she was, which was probably why he was acting more irascible than normal.

"Davenport."

"I never said he was. He asked me to come in today, not the other way around."

"What for?"

"Why don't you ask him?" she asked, stopping and turning to look at him with a raised eyebrow.

He frowned, nearly plowing into her when she stopped, but he kept quiet for once.

"Didn't think so. Now, if you don't mind, he's waiting for me," she said, heading toward the office, leaving Balcher behind with a disgruntled expression on his face.

She knocked once and went in. "What's up?" she asked Davenport when he raised his head from the paperwork he was perusing.

"Shut the door."

She did as he asked and sat down in the leather chair opposite his desk. Three of her could have fit into that chair. "This sounds serious," she said, sitting on the edge of the seat. If she leaned back, she imagined falling into a crack of the cavernous chair and never being found again.

He put his elbows on his desk and rested his chin in his hands. "It's a sensitive situation. We have a woman in custody who's working with her husband in a kidnapping scam. She knows where he is, but she's not talking. We've been given a deadline. If we don't let the wife go in two hours, he'll kill the child. The little girl belongs to a whale from Caesar's Palace. She was snatched right out from under the nanny while the parents were in the casino. Security cameras got everything—that's how we caught up with the wife—but her husband got away."

"And you want me to do what?"

"Bump into her when we let her out of the interrogation room to go to the bathroom. She's been screeching about going to the can for the last half hour. We were waiting on you to get here," he said pointedly. "See if you can get anything out of her, a location or anything else that could help us pinpoint where the husband is."

She frowned. "She might not know where he is."

"She knows. Besides, even if I'm wrong, you can see other things if the contact is long enough, can't you?"

"Maybe. What am I supposed to do? Hold her hand on the way to the john?" she asked, perturbed.

"No. Just bump into her with a cup of coffee. Then you can wipe it off of her or something."

She asked, "Is this legal?"

"Why not? Telepathy is not legally recognized by the state and since we're not going to tell anyone what we're up to, there's no reason for you to be worried."

She leaned forward. "Jim, have you ever really thought about some of the things we've done? I mean, ethically, if not technically, this breaks all kinds of privacy laws."

He leaned back, keeping the distance between them at a status quo. "And how many lives have been saved? And what about that one guy that was innocent that you helped free when the evidence was overwhelming that he was guilty?" he asked, looking at her appealingly.

She frowned, the all too familiar sensation of being used beginning to get her back up. In hindsight—and in frustration, she had to admit—it seemed that he always threw a little flirtation into these sessions, intentionally using her crush on him against her.

It would take an extraordinarily careful and deliberate man to maintain the distance that Jim consistently kept between them over the last three years. She could not remember him ever touching her, not once, even to shake her hand. She had been so worried on her own behalf about touching others that she had not fully realized his reticence until now.

"Come on, Spooky. There's a little girl's life at stake. You're not going to let her down, are you?" He always looked so earnest, his handsome face so seemingly open and beseeching. It was a face that was damned near impossible to say no to. Not to mention that he was right. Finding that little girl alive was not only the logical, but the moral thing to do.

"Yeah...okay," she said hesitantly. "I'll do it. But after this, we need to have a serious talk about what we're doing from this point on. If you want my help with missing persons cases, you got it. But I'm getting uncomfortable about some of this other stuff."

She saw the smallest tick on his upper lip. Then he smiled. "Whatever you say. Come on." He jumped up and led her out of his office and to a position in the hallway near the bathroom. He glanced at his watch and then he handed her a cup of lukewarm coffee that he had carried from his office. "She's wearing a blue blouse and she'll be escorted by Sandy. Sandy knows what's going to happen but she doesn't know why. Just do what you can," he said and walked off.

She frowned uneasily as she waited in the hallway. Balcher was watching her from across the room and that unsettled her even more. She tried to ignore him.

She was still exhausted from last night's trip to the point that she was almost shaking. Jim had not commented on her appearance. It obviously did not concern him. If she still had any questions about what she meant to him, that should have answered them.

She heard the bathroom door open and Sandy came out leading a woman by the elbow. The woman was sixty, if she was a day. She had bottle-blond hair and skin that had seen more sun than was healthy.

She looked like a piece of human trash who was barely holding onto the dreams this town promised by her long, red, fake fingernails. Desperation and denial clouded her eyes as they sunk behind the clownish makeup she wore. On first glance, she didn't necessarily look like a woman that would kidnap a child, but this town did strange things to people.

Spooky pushed away from the wall where she had been resting and headed towards the woman. Sandy moved to the left side of the hall leaving her directly in line with the suspect. Acting as if she were drunk—not a hard thing to do since she was not entirely steady on her feet this morning—she staggered into the woman letting the coffee spill down the woman's blouse, the wetness highlighting the immense cleavage of the woman's breasts. She felt a momentary flutter of envy before going into action.

"Oh, crap!" she slurred, grabbing the woman's arm and pulling her own loose t-shirt away from her waist to use as a makeshift towel. She swiped at the dripping coffee on the woman's blouse. "I'm sorry! Let me help you—"

"Get your filthy hands off of me!" the woman screeched, earning the attention of everyone within shouting distance. Spooky barely heard her. She didn't feel the woman's birdlike talons on her wrist, either.

Images began to hit her, slamming into her brain painfully. The woman tried harder to pull Spooky's hand off of her arm, but the contact only enhanced the barrage of images that pelted Spooky's mind. After about seven seconds, which felt like an eternity, she had gotten what they needed and much more.

She let go of the woman and nearly fell to the floor—*would* have fallen to the floor except for the hands that caught her. She fought against the touch, but it was too late. The images started again.

She was in a warehouse. Bullets pinged all around her as they ricocheted off the surface of the barrels stacked high against the walls. A couple hit close to her and she was petrified. Out of the corner of her eye, she saw a man jump out from behind the boxes they were using as a barricade and take off. She was up and running after him, screaming at the top of her lungs for him to come back.

The man was hit by gunfire and the reel of images wound down to slow motion in her head. The impact from the bullets lifted him off his feet, the look of surprise on his face almost comical. He hung there in the air forever it seemed, but it couldn't have been because the next image that assaulted her brain was of him hitting the cement floor hard. Blood spurted from the man's back and she screamed in pain. Not because she was hit too, but because he was her best friend, her partner. She grabbed him up amidst bullets pelting the ground around her and dragged him back to the barricade. She—

The contact ended. He let go and she slumped to the floor.

"Is she drunk?" a voice asked from above, but she could not look up to see who was talking. She felt drunk, dog tired, hugging the toilet, drunk. Actually, that would have been an improvement. A hand reached down to help her up and she skittered away from it. She could not touch anyone else just now. She could not bear it.

"Don't," she said, crawling a short distance away before holding onto the wall and pulling herself to her feet. Her gaze swam around the faces nearby before resting on one. Balcher's. He looked concerned. All the other faces were either full of pity or full of disgust. She was surprised. Not by the pity and disgust on most of the faces, but by the concern from Balcher.

She moved further away. "I'm all right. It's just the flu," she mumbled before heading for the bathroom. She barely made it there before she collapsed again. She sat on the cold tile floor for nearly thirty minutes before Sandy came looking for her.

"You all right?" the officer asked. "Davenport wants to see you, pronto."

Spooky saw the skeptical expression on the woman's face and she could not help wishing she were at home. The thought of going out of that door and back through that gauntlet of people actually frightened her.

She was too tired for this. Too raw. She was used to using her gifts maybe once a week. Three times in less than twenty-four hours was a record for her, especially with a trip being one of them. She needed to get home.

"Tell him to call me at home," she said, getting shakily to her feet. "I can tell him everything he wants to know from there." She turned away from the woman's astonished expression and opened the bathroom door. There was not anyone standing close by so she left the safety of the bathroom, focusing mightily on getting out of the building without touching anyone else.

She got a few strange glances as she furtively moved through the station, but five minutes later she was in her car and on her way home. She reached into the small, hidden storage compartment she had installed under the dashboard for her billfold. She never took it out of the car. If she needed money, it would always be there. She never knew when she would need to 'trip' and she could not afford to leave behind any identification after one of her trips. She kept a set of spare keys hidden under the car as well. Just in case. There were certainly drawbacks to teleportation.

She stopped at a Taco Bell and ordered five hard-shell taco supremes, an order of nachos supreme, a Mexican pizza and a large Pepsi. Most of the tacos were gone by the time she drove into her driveway. The rest she took inside to finish off at her leisure.

The phone was ringing as she opened the front door. She ran to answer it, dropping the bag of food onto the couch beside her.

"Hi, Jim," she said, sinking down into the cushions of the couch in exhaustion. She pulled the carton of nachos out of the bag while she listened to him vent for two minutes. She was munching on one of them when he finally let up.

"Are you ready to hear what I know yet? Or do you want to chew me out a little while longer?"

She heard his sigh over the phone. "I'm listening," he grunted.

"The woman's husband stashed the kid in one of the empty hotel rooms right there at the Caesar. Room 713. They had help. Penny, one of the maids from the hotel, is watching her."

"Well, I'll be damned," he grunted. "We searched the hotel but didn't find her. I knew it had to be something like that. The hotel's security cameras didn't catch them leaving with the child, but we thought they got her out in a trunk or something. Gotta go," he grumbled and hung up.

"And thank you for coming down to help, Spooky, especially since you were so sick and all," she mumbled sarcastically at the empty line before she hung the phone up. "Jim Davenport, you're starting to piss me off."

She picked up the TV remote and clicked the set on. She channel surfed until she found the Sci-Fi channel. Her unique abilities made her feel like an alien, especially after a day like today. The shows on that channel sometimes eased some of those feelings, giving her a glimmer of hope that there were others like her out in the world if she could only find them. She was an abnormality, a misfit, a circus freak.

Today it was not working. She only felt worse as she watched a movie that had the government chasing after a little girl that could change people's lives by the touch of her hand. Every time she considered the possibility of letting someone in on her secret, she was reminded of what would happen if she did. She could only imagine what the United States Government would do to a woman that could teleport.

She was so lonely. A tear spilled onto her cheek and she wiped it away angrily. She was not going to let self-pity and Davenport's possible motives for befriending her get to her. She had to face it. She was an investigative tool to him, one that increased his ratio for solving cases, thereby making him look good.

What did it matter? His motives for using her were inconsequential. Whether he did it to help people or to help himself should not matter as long as the public was served. What other purpose could there be for someone like her?

She finished the nachos and started on the Mexican pizza. Her stomach nearly groaned at the punishment but she needed the fuel. Trippin' was not the only thing that caused her metabolism to spike. Her visions did the same thing albeit in a less spectacular manner. She was probably down another pound or two from this morning. She did not want to look at the scales. It was too depressing.

To get her mind off her own problems, she thought about what she saw when she touched that woman this morning. It was just another pitiful story of human greed and lost hope. The woman and her husband came to live in Las Vegas after he retired. It was her idea. She wanted a chance at the excitement and glamour that had been missing from her life in New Mexico. Since moving here, she'd had a few lovers her husband was not aware of and lost loads of money at the blackjack tables and the slot machines. Nearly all of her husband's retirement money was gone in a year. That was when her new buddy, the Caesars Palace maid by the name of Penny something or other, mentioned the 'whale' that was throwing money around at the casino like it grew on trees. That was not an unusual happening at the casino, but Penny liked to brag.

The idea of a man that rich fascinated the woman. In her mind, she deserved a man like that, someone rich and handsome who would spoil her endlessly. She tried to friendly up with the whale, but the only thing her gave her was a pitying look.

Incensed, the woman came up with a plan to get back at him and to get some of his money while she was at it. She did not have a hard time convincing her sucker of a husband to go along with it, either.

With such inherent stupidity, Spooky was amazed that they got so far in their plan. She did not fear for the child. The weak husband she saw in the woman's mind would not have gone through with his threat. That was why she felt safe to come home before she filled Jim in on the girl's whereabouts.

With the food gone, she turned off the movie already knowing the ending by heart. The little girl would get away only to be looking over her shoulder for the rest of her life and wondering if the next stop in the road would be her last or if the next friend she made was not really who they said they were. It was a paranoiac view of life but one that Spooky would always live with.

She got up from the couch, went to her bedroom and crawled under the covers of her unmade bed. Using the bedside phone, she called her contact at the Radicom office and let him know what had happened the night before. He informed her that his staff had found some clothes and a backpack in its outer office, but no camera. She heard the curiosity in his voice, but she didn't satisfy it. She just told him that she'd have to do some more tracking before she could finish the case. He wasn't happy with the information, but right at the moment, she didn't care.

She felt like she could sleep for a week. She wouldn't, but it was a comforting thought. In sleep, she had dreams. In dream, she had friends...*and lovers*. She almost smiled as she closed her eyes, but then Balcher's face inserted itself into her thoughts. Now why would she think of him and lovers in the same thought? The idea was ludicrous, but as her eyes drooped, he followed her into her dreams.

Chapter Three

Michael Balcher hit the snack machine in frustration. His Mars bar was stuck on the metal spiral thingamagimmy.

"Whatsomatta, Mikey? Machine holding your candy bar hostage?" his best buddy and partner, Zack Mangoni, snickered as he came up behind him.

"Yeah," he grunted, pulling another dollar bill out of his pocket and trying to flatten it out so that the machine would take it. He put the bill into the slot and the machine spit it back out. He glowered at the machine and then turned the bill around and tried it again. It worked. He pushed J4 and this time the Mars bar fell down into the slot bringing the other one with it. He grabbed them both.

"You gonna eat both of those?" his skinny partner asked.

"Yeah. What about it?" he grunted, a fierce look on his face.

The look did not daunt Zack for a second. "I hesitate to say this, buddy, but you don't need two candy bars. Hell, you don't even need one," he said looking pointedly towards Balcher's stomach.

"Who asked you?" Balcher grumbled, heading back to his desk.

"Just bein' a friend. Friends don't let friends drive drunk, and friends don't let fat friends eat junk," Zack said laughing at his rhyme.

Balcher rolled his eyes. "I am not fat. But, again I ask, what's it to you?"

"No skin off my nose," Zack said, hands in the air, all innocent. "I just don't see you out dating these days. How long has it been since you've done the nasty? Huh? If you keep up this candy bar habit, those few pounds around your waist are gonna turn into trouble and they'll kill you *and* your sex life."

"And I suppose the women are flocking to your skinny ass, huh? The only gal—and I use that term lightly—I've seen interested in you lately was Francesca from the Mirage," he said referring to the transsexual bar tender they interrogated last week.

"At least somebody's interested. You can't even get Spooky to look your way."

"I'm not interested in her that way," Balcher lied threateningly. He was still trying to figure out how she got past him last night. He had waited in that danged parking lot until the sun came up and her car was still there. Of course, missing a night's sleep wasn't helping his disposition, either. "I'm just trying to figure out what's going on between her and the captain."

"Yeah? What's up with that? Capt'n Wonderful wouldn't give her the time of day if she wasn't doin' something to make him look good," Zack said, wiggling his eyebrows.

"That's what I mean. Wonderboy's been crapping gold since he hooked up with Spooky and I want to know why. What are they up to? And, if it is on the up and up, then why doesn't he let us in on it? Something's fishy. Something's really fishy. Especially after this morning."

"What? Because 'the Spookster' came in here drunk?"

"She wasn't drunk. I smelled her breath. Maybe she was sick like she said. But something else is bothering me. How come Davenport all of a sudden knows to send Benny and Eve over to the Palace to find that little girl? He knew the exact room number, too. I heard Eve talking about it when they got back. The girl was right where Davenport said she'd be. All this happened right after Spooky had a run-in with the wife of the suspect," he murmured in frustration.

"Spooky's a good P.I. Maybe she heard something from one of her sources."

"You weren't listening, Zachary." Balcher always used his partner's entire first name when he was pissed at him. "Spooky was waiting right there in that hall for that woman to come out of the bathroom. Davenport placed her there. I saw him. He gave her the coffee she spilled on the woman. Spooky stood there until the woman came out and then she headed right for her.

"I was right behind her when she drenched that bleached-blond bimbo with the coffee and grabbed her arm. You should have heard that witch screeching while she tried to pry Spooky's hand off her arm. All the while Spooky has this strange expression on her face. It was like she was a million miles away and seeing something the rest of us couldn't. When she finally let go, she nearly hit the floor. I grabbed her and I saw that expression again. It scared me so bad, I let her go. Then she did hit the floor."

"What're saying, Mikey? You ain't thinking the Spookster...er, Spooky is a psychic, are you?"

Balcher almost smiled at the expression on Zack's face. "Something like that, yeah. Nothing else makes sense. And it would explain the name. I've been checking up on her. Her real name is Sarah Knight. Spooky is just a nickname. She said it was a Halloween prank that earned her the nickname, but I'm not so sure."

"But a psychic? That's out there, man," Zack said as he whistled the *Twilight Zone* theme music.

"Maybe, Zack. Maybe it is. But something's up. Her name's not all I checked on. I've checked out some of her cases, too, talked to some of her clients. They're all closed mouthed about her, except to say that she's good at what she does. She finds missing persons that no one else can find. Cold cases, too. And she does it fast. Think about it, Zack. She's twenty-six years old and has become one of Vegas's leading P.I.s. She makes top dollar from what I hear. She works alone, no partners or leg men. Works out of an office in her house. It adds up to me."

"To being a psychic?" Zack smirked.

"So don't believe me. You come up with an explanation for Davenport's incredible good luck over the last three years and I'll bow to your expertise. I never gave psychics much thought before, but something about Spooky's been bothering me for a long time."

Zack snorted. "Tell me about it. I thought you had the hots for her.

It's good to know my best bud hasn't lost all his marbles. I have to tell you, Mikey, I was gettin' worried about you. You could have any woman you wanted. You're not a bad lookin' galoot."

Balcher felt uncomfortable with the way the conversation was going. He knew how most of the guys at the station felt about Spooky. They tolerated her for the captain's sake, but talked about her mercilessly. He did some of his own talking about her at first. She was one of the weirdest chicks he had ever met. But somewhere along the line, he began to feel sorry for her.

She seemed so isolated. She stood back from people when they talked to her and never instigated a conversation on her own. She looked like she was one step away from starvation. Her clothes were clean, but always loose. She wasn't really ugly, just way too thin. She had soulful gray eyes. She could be a real looker if she wore a little makeup and tried more form-fitting clothes.

When he was investigating her, he looked for family and friends. He found out that her ex-con mother was deceased, a drug overdose when Spooky was eighteen. She had no father listed, no siblings, no aunts, uncles, or grandparents that he could find. This week, as he kept her under surveillance, he looked for friends, particularly boyfriends, but he never saw her with anyone. She stayed home every night, except last night, and the flicker of the TV screen was the only company she had except for the takeout delivery men he saw at her door every evening. At least he knew she was eating.

He sighed. He was nearly obsessed with the woman, but he was not about to admit that to Zack. He couldn't figure out why she got to him so bad. Maybe it was because of her loneliness. He felt it, too, this feeling of being different, of not conforming to the ideals of those around him. He was not what everyone thought he was. At six-foot, five, two hundred and fifty-five pounds, and a face that looked like it had taken one too many punches, not to mention a voice right out of a Rocky movie, he was thought to be a thick-headed piece of muscle. No one expected his intelligence, his sensitivity to others. When they saw it, they ignored it as an oddity.

As different as he was from most people, he didn't imagine it came close to matching the isolation Spooky felt if he was right about her. After today, he was almost positive that she was psychic. She must be what they called a touch telepath. That is why she had to hold onto that woman to get the information Davenport wanted.

He couldn't believe that he freaked out and let her fall when she went into that trance. He shouldn't have dropped her like he did, but God knows he wished he knew what she had seen. He also wished that he had helped her out of the station instead of just standing there gawking like the rest of them when she stumbled to the bathroom.

He was ashamed of himself. Sure, he gave her a hard time when she came to the station. It was the only way he could think of to talk to her. If he tried the sensitive approach, she wouldn't have responded. He was sure of that. Inside the isolation, he saw a will of iron. But to let her walk alone though that gauntlet of derision this morning was despicable.

He shook it off. He would make it up to her if she would let him. Something told him that she was headed for a fall and he did not mean just a quick trip to the floor. She had trouble looming in her future. Davenport was not being honorable in his use of her. Next time, Balcher determined, he would be there for her.

Chapter Four

"I can't believe I'm wastin' my day off like this," Zack grumbled as they passed the lion cage inside the gargantuan indoor zoo exhibit. Only a Las Vegas Casino could attempt something this outrageous and get away with it.

"Would you quit griping? I didn't force you to come along. You're the one that insisted," Balcher muttered in irritation. Zack was a dear friend, but sometimes he could test the patience of a saint, a category in which Balcher definitely did not fit.

Balcher would have preferred to do this alone, but since he opened his mouth the other day about Spooky's possible psychic abilities and his admitted interest in her, Zack was sticking to him like glue.

"You didn't say we'd need to be fumigated," Zack said waving a hand in front of his nose and his face was screwed up like he'd just bitten into a lemon.

"It's not that bad," Balcher growled, keeping an eye on Spooky who was talking with some man that she'd met up with a half hour ago. The meeting looked intense, the man waving his hands excitedly at times. Spooky was true to form, keeping her distance and composure, but listening intently. Balcher thought he could get closer without her noticing so he headed for the monkey's cage, which was the last obstacle between him and his target.

"Oh, man, I hate monkeys," Zack mumbled as they stopped at the cage.

"Just try to look interested," Balcher said, his attention on Spooky.

Zack stared at the chimpanzees doing his best impression of looking interested. The big monkey in the back didn't appreciate the interest. He loped to the bars, bared his teeth at Zack and screeched.

Zack jumped back. "I told you, man, I hate monkeys. And they don't like me much, neither."

Balcher glared at him impatiently. "Keep it down, idiot!"

"I didn't do nothing!" Zack spluttered.

Balcher turned back to make sure Spooky had not spotted them. She was still in deep conversation with the man. The guy looked a little familiar to Balcher. He was obviously well to do. The suit was expensive, not to mention the bling-bling the guy was sporting.

"Don't this guy look familiar to—" He turned to Zack only to find him making faces at the monkey. The monkey bared his teeth and stuck out his chin. Zack bared his teeth and stuck out his chin in response. The contest went on between them for about ten seconds, all the while the monkey was getting madder and madder if the screeching was anything to go by.

"Zack, will you stop it!" he growled, worried that the monkey's outburst was going to gain Spooky's attention. "She's gonna see us!"

All of a sudden the monkey grabbed his chest and fell over. He hit the floor, eyes and mouth wide open but his chest was not moving up and down. No evidence of life.

"Are you crazy?" hissed Balcher, pulling Zack away from the cage before anyone could come running up and spoil his surveillance of Spooky.

"I couldn't let that monkey be the boss of me!" Zack defended himself.

"Yeah? I bet that damned monkey thought the same thing," Balcher said trying to hide his hulk behind a column near the lion's cage. He wished he could disappear into the floor. "You just killed that monkey," he growled at his partner.

"It's not my fault!" Zack whispered vehemently.

"Let's get out of here before she comes," Balcher ordered as he dragged his friend towards the entrance of the casino, his head facing Zack and not watching where he was going.

He looked up just in time to keep from running into her.

"Balcher," she murmured. "Funny seeing you here."

"Sa—uh, Spooky," he stuttered as he stared at her in awe. Her nice outfit and makeup looked pretty good up close and it almost threw him for a moment, causing him to slip up on her name. "Zack and I just came to see the zoo exhibit."

"Really?" she questioned innocently. "Which one? The monkeys, perhaps?"

"Uh, yeah. The monkeys. They're kind of cute, don't you think?" he stammered.

"All of them except for the dead one, yeah," she agreed with a smirk.

"That wasn't my fault!" Zack spluttered.

"I'm not so sure about that," Spooky murmured, moving her attention from Balcher to Zack. "It looks pretty suspicious to me. I think someone should call the police and report a murder."

"I didn't murder that monkey!" shouted Zack, his skin turning all shades of colors.

"Then how'd he get dead?" she asked.

"I—" Zack started, but stopped abruptly when Casino security headed their way. "Oh, shoot!" he groaned.

The guys from security barely had time to stop before them when Zack blurted out, "He had a heart attack. I didn't do it!"

The older guy looked at his partner in confusion and then back at Zack. "You didn't do what?"

Zack rolled his eyes. "I didn't kill that monkey!"

"What monkey?" asked the younger security officer.

Zack pointed at the cage in question and was surprised to see that all of the monkeys were up and about.

The older guy, Paul Brewer, laughed. "Oh, you mean Henry? He does that to a lot of people. Grabbed his heart and fell over, right?"

"You mean that danged monkey is alive?" Zack asked, looking like he wanted to go over there and kill the monkey again. Then he thought better of it. "If you ain't here about the monkey then what do you want?" he groused to the two men.

"Mr. Harrell would like to speak with Ms. Knight again," Brewer said, speaking of the manager of the casino and looking pointedly at Spooky. "In his office and right away."

Balcher realized that the guy he'd seen Spooky with earlier must be the owner, or at least, the manager of the casino because those words sounded like an order. And it looked to Balcher as if Spooky took it as one.

Spooky nodded and followed the two men to the special elevator that went to Harrell's office. Balcher knew it was not really an office. It was a floor specially set aside for electronics and surveillance equipment that kept the casino running as smoothly as it did. This much money had to be watched constantly, not to mention the patrons, some of whom might try to fake an injury or a fall and sue the management.

Balcher was still curious about what Harrell wanted from Spooky and he felt a momentary flash of irritation at the way Harrell ordered Spooky around. It was the same kind of irritation he felt towards Davenport back at the station.

He shrugged it off. She did work for a lot of people in this town. God knows these casino people were tight fisted with their money. If they thought a psychic could tell them if a card counter was at work in their establishment, then they would put her to good use.

At least it got her off of his back. For the moment, anyway.

He grabbed Zack's elbow and pulled him outside. "Great help you turned out to be," he muttered. "Next time, just bring a neon sign with you that says, *'Look at me. I'm following you!'*"

"If she was really a psychic, then she would have already known we was there, wouldn't she?" Zack responded sarcastically.

"Were there," Balcher corrected him.

"What?"

"She would have known we *were* there," Balcher said disgruntled.

"Ain't that what I said?"

"Never mind," Balcher said rolling his eyes. "It doesn't work like that."

"How do you know how it works?"

"Just take my word for it," he growled. "I don't have the time, or the inclination to explain it all to you. Just keep this in mind. She has to touch something to get her visions. She doesn't just read minds. At least, I hope to God she doesn't," he said crossing his heart.

"You're really starting to believe all of this, aren't you?" Zack said in amazement.

"Don't go hunting up the men in white suits just yet. I still have a lot to figure out before I commit to my theory. But it's starting to look real to me."

"Mikey, you're taking all this *way* too seriously. I mean, even if the captain is using her 'so called' abilities, what's it to us? He'll get the promotion he wants and then he'll be out of our hair. That's a good thing."

Balcher shrugged. "He's using her and I don't like it. She's gonna get hurt."

"So? Why do you care?"

"Because I'm a human being, idiot. Unlike some people I know," he said pointedly as he eyed his best friend.

Zack shook his head. "You're in for a hard fall, my friend."

Balcher gave up trying to hide his feelings. "I'm already on the way down, man," he admitted. He held up a hand to stop his friend from replying. "You don't need to say it. I know she won't be easy, but I can't help it. I have to know what's up with her. I can't leave it alone."

"Your funeral," Zack murmured.

Balcher felt a chill run down his spine. The words seemed prophetic. "Let's hope not, Zack. Let's just get out of here. She's probably already up there with Harrell in that observation room. I don't want her to see us."

He headed out of the door and into the sunshine of the bright, hot day. Las Vegas in July was like an oven, but at least there was very little humidity today. The transition from the loud, glittering, air-conditioned interior of the casino to the relatively quiet, bright light of day was almost like stepping into another world.

Actually, since the day before yesterday when Spooky touched him and went into that trance, he felt weird no matter where he went. His suspicions and obsessions about Spooky have tilted his world sideways and he was having trouble knowing which way was up.

And, he had the strangest feeling that she *would* eventually be the death of him.

Chapter Five

Spooky watched the detectives leave the casino. It appeared that Balcher was no longer satisfied with haranguing her at the station. He had taken it a step further and was following her now. The last few days she'd felt danger in the air around her and couldn't help wondering if he was part of it, or if he would unintentionally be harmed by it. And ever since she saw the compassion in his eyes the day before yesterday, she had begun questioning the parameters of the connection they shared.

There was some kind of a bond building there, no doubt about it. Before, she only felt murky webs of antagonism and an intellectual interest coming from him. Now, she wasn't so sure. With what she saw in his head the other day—the emotional pain of losing a partner and what it did to him—and now with catching him following her, she felt the connection between them shift dramatically.

He was weaving himself around her, and she didn't know how to stop him.

"Can you tell how he's doing it?"

Harrell's question brought her mind back to the situation at hand. "I'll have to get close to him before I can tell you anything." She looked at the monitor that was honed in on a blackjack table near the center of the casino. There were four players and a dealer at the table, but she couldn't make out much at this distance. She had worked with Winston Harrell—Win for short, although she preferred to call him Harrell—on several jobs before and he knew how she worked. He didn't necessarily know that she was psychic, but he trusted her conclusions and really didn't care how she came to them. "How long have you been following him?" she asked.

His eyes hadn't moved from the screen. "The last day and a half. He's won over a hundred thousand, so far. He's either fantastically lucky or something's up."

She watched the guy in question. Something about his posture looked familiar. "Nobody's that lucky," she murmured.

He nodded. "Get back to me when you know. If the guy is counting cards, then he's good at it because he doesn't appear to be paying much attention to the dealer."

"He could have a partner that's doing the counting. The partner could be losing intentionally to keep from raising suspicions, and then signaling him when to bet or not bet," she said.

He shook his head negatively. "We've watched him. He goes from table to table and nobody goes with him. He's never played a table with the same people more than once."

She gave him a level look. "You think he's psychic, don't you?"

He finally took his eyes of the screen and looked squarely at her. "I think if anyone could figure that out, you could."

He didn't come right out and ask her if she was psychic, but it was as good as said. She smiled. "Maybe."

"Just don't let me catch *you* at my tables," he said with a lop-sided grin that would have looked natural on a shark.

Spooky took the warning in stride. "How about the slots?" she asked with a raised eyebrow.

"They're fair game. If you feel led to play one, no skin off my nose," he said, confirming what everybody knew about slot machines. They were scheduled to pay off certain amounts at certain times and it didn't matter to the management who was playing them at the time.

"Good to know," she said with a wave as she was leaving. This job was going to be quick money. It always was. One touch of the table and she could read the whole group playing on it.

She walked into the loud room focusing intently on her target. She had to concentrate hard not to let the emotions of the hordes of people around her to get into her head. She normally couldn't read people without touching them, but casinos were desperate places for a lot of people and desperation shouted out at her louder than the raucous sounds of the slot machines. People here had dreams of getting rich, hitting it big, but most of them went home without next month's rent or car payment. She had made it a rule to never step foot in the casinos except for when she was on a job. Even if she could read a slot machine and tell when it was about to hit, she couldn't bear the thought of taking that prize from one of the other desperate people putting their quarters, dimes or dollars into the machine. It wouldn't be fair.

She came around the last row of slot machines and the space opened up to a group of ten blackjack tables. She saw her target at the third table down. She headed for the table and settled into a chair at the other end away from her target without giving him a glance. She had dressed a little better for this job because she knew Harrell wouldn't allow her into his casino in what she normally wore. She was actually wearing makeup and her hair was twisted up with a barrette at the back of her head. She had jeweled earrings dangling from her ears and a shimmering gold charm bracelet on her thin wrist. Her black dress was last years model and loose on her from the nine pounds she recently lost, but she'd cinched it in with a wide gold-weave belt. She looked decent enough to not stand out.

For a moment, she flashed back to Balcher's look of astonishment when she ran into him earlier. He had never seen her fixed up before. As much as she had wanted to impress Captain Jim, she always felt that dressing up for him would only amuse him. She was not that desperate.

But Balcher's interest disturbed her. After the astonishment, she could have sworn she saw a gleam of hunger in his eyes. That flash of emotion formed yet another strand of the web in their connection, making it stronger. She felt tethered to him in a way she had never connected before.

"Place your bets."

The dealer's words brought her out of her introspection. She usually had no trouble concentrating on her work, but lately she's been distracted. All because of Balcher.

She placed a few of her chips on the table and then rested her hand on the green velvet surface of the table. She immediately felt the connection. The man to her right was amusedly bored. He wasn't winning much, but he wasn't losing much, either. Apparently, he was here with the woman beside him. She was a beautiful woman and new to gambling. Her excitement was coming through loud and clear. The gentleman on the other side of her was worried about his wife who had gone to the ladies room nearly an hour ago and had not come back yet. He was getting ready to go look for her after this hand.

She wasn't getting much from the man at the other end of the table. She finally looked up and found him staring straight at her. She nodded and smiled briefly at the casually dressed, but intensely alert, man in what she hoped was a nonchalant manner and then touched her cards to indicate for the dealer to 'hit' her. He laid a nine of hearts down beside her two of clubs and eight of spades. She had nineteen. She glanced back towards her target. He was still staring at her. She almost looked away and then she began to feel a tingling in her fingers where they touched the table. The man smiled and turned towards the dealer and she saw him in profile for the first time.

It was him!

She felt a jolt of electricity run through her fingertips and she snatched them away from the table. Her eyes dilated as she stared at him.

Danger.

It was as clear as anything she had ever felt before. The same danger she felt the night she tripped at the Radicom office. She couldn't read anything else from him. Just that instinctual feeling that she was in the line of fire.

From somewhere far off, she heard the dealer say she'd won. She pulled the chips towards her and grabbed them up. She left the table and headed fast for the elevator. She ran into the enclosure and pressed the button to close the door. She looked out into the crowd beyond the elevator's doors and she saw him. He was standing there, barely ten feet away, smiling at her. It was not a nice smile, more of a sarcastic smirk. The doors of the elevator closed, slowly closing off her view of him and she was shaking as she leaned back against the mirrored back wall. For a moment she was frozen, and then with a trembling hand she pressed the key Harrell gave her into the special slot and the elevator started up towards the fifth floor.

She saw Harrell across the room and headed in his direction. "Who is he?" she asked him forcefully.

"You mean—"

"The man. Who is he?"

"Nicholas Brandson, from California. Why?"

"I've come across him on another case, something I can't talk about. I think he was here to get my attention. This doesn't have anything to do with gambling. Somehow, he's figured out that I've worked for you in the past and he was here trying to draw me out."

"But how was he winning—"

She interrupted him, "I couldn't get a good read because he wasn't concentrating on the money. He was after me," she said, and then grimaced when she realized what she had just admitted to the man in front of her. "If he is who I think he is, he's got some powerful electronic toys at his disposal. He could have some ultra cool contact lenses that can see through the cards or something. I don't know." She paced back in forth in front of him nervously as her imagination flew off in several directions. How did that guy know who she was? And how did he know he could find her here?

"Then we'll just bring him up here and have a go at him with our electronic sensor device—"

"No!" she nearly shouted, stopping in front of him. "Besides, you won't find anything on him now. He's already got what he came here for."

Harrell's eyes narrowed. "You?"

Spooky nodded. "You've been paying me through that corporation I set up, right? I mean, there's no mention of my real name anywhere on your books, is there?"

"No. But you're in my rolodex," he admitted with a grim look. "But I'll take care of that right now. Nobody else here knows your real name or phone number. They just know you as Spooky."

Spooky was shaking so hard inside that it was difficult to think. She had planned in advance for something like this. No one knew her home address, but several people had her cell phone number which was forwarded to her home number when she was not out on a case. Her bank accounts were in her corporate name, so was her car, and the only address associated with her legal name was a P.O. Box at a downtown Post Office.

She wanted desperately to 'trip' home right now. If the man knew what she drove, then he could be outside right now waiting for her to head home. But she couldn't. She was still too weak from the last time.

"Can I stay here for a little while?" she asked Harrell.

"Sure, as long as you want." He shrugged. "The guy's gone anyway. He left the tables right after you did and I haven't seen him since."

She nodded her appreciation and then flipped her cell phone open. She had no signal. Considering the amount of electronics in the room, that made sense. "Can I use one of your phones?"

"Sure, go ahead. I'll be in my office if you need anything," he said and then left her to her business.

She called Davenport's direct line. "Captain Davenport, please," she asked when someone else picked up.

"He's not in at the moment, can I take a message?"

"When will he be in?"

"Not for the rest of the day. Who's this? Maybe someone else can help you?" the voice on the other end said.

"What about Detective Balcher," she asked, hating to bring him into this, but at the moment, she didn't have any other choice.

"This is his day off, ma'am. Would you like to speak with another detective?" the man said, his voice beginning to sound a bit irritated.

Spooky hung up. She'd have to chance it. She headed for the elevator and hit the button for five different floors including the thirtieth floor. If the man had been watching, he'd have to have seen that she stopped on the fifth floor earlier, so going up first was the only smart thing to do. He wouldn't be expecting her to come down from the penthouse floor.

*   *   *

Balcher found himself headed back to the casino after he dropped Zack off at home. Spooky was not stupid, she had to know that he'd been following her. He needed to find her fast while he still had a head start on her. He'd felt really strange since the other day when he held her for those few moments. It wasn't just worry of what she'd seen inside of him while they were touching—he knew she'd seen something from deep down inside him, something that he'd kept hidden from the outside world—but he'd felt something from her catch hold inside him at the same time. They had connected in some strange, unimaginable way.

He almost laughed out loud at the notion. If Granny Odelle had still been alive, she would have given him fits if he'd told her about all of this. Granny had the sight, or at least that's what she told people as she read their fortunes down by the bayou in Louisiana all those years ago. Yes, Granny would have made a huge deal out of all this craziness that was going on in his life because of Spooky.

And maybe, for the first time, he would have listened to her.

He pulled into the drive for the casino and lucked up in finding a parking spot close to the entrance as a car was just pulling out. He was beginning to feel a sense of urgency to find Spooky. The hairs on the back of his neck stood up as he entered the sparkling interior of the casino and he knew he was close. At first, he didn't know where to start, but something, a weird urging, edged him towards the bank of elevators.

That was fine by him. The last he saw of Spooky, she was headed towards the fifth floor to see the head honcho of the casino. He made his way to the red carpeted area and was jostled by a few matronly women as they came out of the first available elevator. They were so excited by the sounds of the slot machines, they barely gave him a glance, which was unusual because he was so big that most women viewed him with awe and generally steered clear of him. With a forced smile, he nodded at them and then went around them into the empty gilded box.

Before he could figure out the electronic panel and determine how he could override the security measures associated with the fifth floor—there was gold button with a key hole in the center of it instead of the lighted buttons that represented every other floor—a man dressed casually in khaki's and some expensive name-brand shirt and navy blue blazer entered the elevator with him. The elevator door closed behind the newcomer leaving the two of them alone in the gaudily decorated space, and the hairs on Balcher's neck stood even taller.

Balcher gave the guy a quick glance and an image of ice flashed into his head. The vision, short though it was, un-nerved him to the point that he openly stared at the stranger. The man was tall, a little over six feet, with white-blond hair and eyes the color of blue ice. His blazer was obviously tailored so Balcher became truly concerned by the tightness across the shoulders of the jacket. The guy had a gun.

Or a really thick wallet, his reasonable mind tried to tell him. It didn't help. The longer he stood there staring, the colder the air in the enclosed elevator got.

Ice man.

The words just popped into his head, and that un-nerved him even more. The man turned towards him. "What floor, buddy?"

"Thirtieth," he said, the number coming out of his mouth without him knowing why he said it. Balcher watched as the man pressed the lighted button stenciled with the number thirty. Then he pressed the button for the twenty-eighth floor and stepped back to lean casually against the wall. This lessened the tension in the space, somewhat. Then they both waited in silence as the elevator started moving upwards.

It was a long ride, the air growing colder as they went higher, and Balcher's skin started crawling again. If he'd been out in the field, he would be ducking by now. That's how loud his instincts were shouting at him to move, to do something. He literally had to strain himself to be still. All of these intuitive feelings were outside of his normal existence and he wasn't sure he could trust them. Maybe he was going crazy?

He certainly couldn't take the man down right there in the elevator. The stranger hadn't committed any overt acts and there was no probable cause for a search, either. The bulge in his jacket most likely was a wallet and not a gun. Hell, the air conditioning could be on the fritz and that might be why it was so cold!

Balcher was not used to such indecisiveness. In the marines, he'd been a bulldozer, a tank, a force to be reckoned with. Same thing with the LVPD. Although he was undoubtedly intelligent, it was his massive body and hard strength that cowed most of the perps he arrested.

The guy standing next to him was no easy prey, either. He felt that in his soul. The man stood with the nonchalance of wolf, wild, but with the wildness leashed, at bay for the moment.

The elevator was now moving swiftly between floors, not stopping to pick up additional passengers. When it finally stopped at the twenty-eighth floor, Balcher let out a deep breath that he hadn't even realized he had been holding.

The man turned towards him and their eyes met briefly. The man nodded, and then left the elevator. Balcher watched the guy start down the hallway, and then the elevator doors slid shut blocking his view. He stood motionless as he headed up to the thirtieth floor, trying to figure out what the hell had just happened. He wasn't planning on getting out on the top floor, he just needed time to figure this out. With a determined sigh, he reached towards the panel to press the button for the sixth floor—he could walk down one floor to get to the observation room if he had to.

The elevator door opened and there stood Spooky.

Chapter Six

"What're you doing here, Balcher?" she asked, surprised. She was even more surprised when he jumped out of the elevator and grabbed her by the arm.

"Come with me," he muttered, scowling.

She jerked her arm away from him, but that didn't stop the tingling. She had another flash from him, something cold and white and dangerous. The images were so close to what was happening in her own head that she didn't yell at him for touching her. She clenched her teeth and reluctantly followed his orders. She had no choice; she needed to find out what he knew.

He marched ahead of her down the hallway until he came to the door marked 'emergency exit' and pushed through it. They found themselves in an empty and dimly lit stairwell. For several long moments, Balcher just stood there, listening and staring down into the stairwell, and then he turned and looked towards the steps that led up to the roof.

"This way," he grunted, and headed up the stairs.

"I'm not going up there with you," she said, backing away and heading back towards the penthouse floor.

He grabbed her arm again. "He's coming," he said, pulling her with him up the stairs.

The physical contact caused a powerful, strumming electricity to run between them, but she didn't ask for any further explanation. Somehow Balcher was mixed up in all of this. He knew who the man was.

He pulled her through the door to the roof and the change from dark to light blinded her. She stumbled up a few steps and then walked out onto the pebbled tile surface of the roof. When her eyes were partially adjusted to the glare, she looked around her. From where she was, she could practically see the whole town with its glitz and glitter against the stark aridness of the desert. It was barely three o'clock in the afternoon but the roof was practically baking in the sun, a shimmering haze rising sultrily in the distance.

She shielded her eyes from the sun with her hand, her other arm still roughly clenched inside of Balcher's huge fist. He dragged her with him to check the other side of the stairway enclosure. For what, she didn't know. When they'd made a complete circuit of the structure and found nothing out of order on the entire rooftop, she pulled her arm away from his grasp. She didn't want the contact, it was too disturbing. At some point, she had stopped getting flashes from him and was beginning to only get a steady hum, like that of an open electrical circuit.

"Why'd you drag me out here?" she asked.

He looked suddenly uncertain of himself, something she would have never imagined if she hadn't seen it for herself. Balcher was nothing if not decisive.

"Don't ask me how I know this, but somebody's after you. A white male, six foot tall, white hair. You know anybody like that?" He looked at her probingly and the look defied her to lie to him.

How'd he know that! She looked away from him, shrinking away from his intrusion into her defenses. "I saw him earlier in the casino. He's been winning a lot of money and Harrell wanted to know how he was doing it," she finally admitted.

"That's not all of it, is it?" he asked.

Spooky walked away from him towards the edge of the roof. She hated heights, but it was preferable to standing so close to Balcher. He was acting almost as if he could see inside of her head. Nobody was allowed to do that!

She felt a little dizzy. There was only a three-foot ledge standing between her and the gleaming pavement of a parking lot nearly thirty floors down and just the thought of it made her stomach clench.

She backed away from the edge and then turned around to face him. He was barely three feet away and the suddenness of seeing him there caused an involuntary step back.

Danger!

Her hands flew back behind her and caught hold of the ledge. She was about to blast the big idiot with a few harsh words when she realized that he was not looking at her, but was turned towards the roof's stairwell. His stance was rigid, like that of a cornered, but dangerous animal. All her instincts went on alert.

She glanced in the direction he was staring and a flash caught her eye. Sun glinted off of something metallic, and then she realized what she was looking at. A man was slowly coming up the steps and out of the shadows of the doorway.

And he had a gun in his hands.

It was the man from the blackjack table; the same man she saw three nights ago at the Radicom offices. The imminent danger she felt from behind, and also from the man coming towards them, made her legs go weak.

Her first instinct was to trip, but she didn't know if she could do it fast enough to stop a bullet from entering her body. And she was worried about Balcher, although the gun, thankfully, was not pointed at him. It was pointed at her, as if the assailant knew she was the significant threat even though Balcher was more than twice her size.

The guy was steadily closing in on her, and Spooky, even in her severely frightened state, was surprised to see that Balcher was moving closer to her as well, placing his bulk between her and that of her attacker.

"Can he teleport as well?" the man asked, stopping about seven feet from them. "I didn't count on there being two of you."

He knows I can teleport! Her brain raced as she tried to put all of this together. He must have found her clothes and backpack the other night, and was intelligent enough to postulate the possibility of teleportation from the evidence at hand. Most people would not have made the jump between empty clothes and teleportation. They would have convinced themselves that she had never been there in the first place because, hey, teleportation was impossible, wasn't it?

Not this man. He was fairly salivating with the possibility. But what did he want from her now?

"How'd you find me?" She asked the first question that came to mind.

"I found your camera. It was not a difficult leap of the imagination to figure out you were a private detective hired to catch me in the act of industrial espionage. So, I asked around town and found out that the *Spooky Knight Detective Agency* had a detective with some questionably spooky resources. A *woma*n detective whose services were highly in demand from all of the casinos that populate this illustrious town. All I had to do was pick one, catch the interest of the management by winning a lot of money, and then wait for you to show up." The man looked smug as he gave her the information.

Spooky was startled at how effortless it was to find her. She'd always thought that she was so careful. "You're a pretty good detective yourself, Mr...?"

"You can call me Ice Man," the man said.

Balcher jerked at the name. How had he known what the man called himself? He was beginning to wonder if this wasn't all just a bad dream, especially when he heard the word 'teleport'. The word drew images of the television show, *Star Trek*. Teleportation was not really possible, was it?

"Ice Man," Spooky murmured. "Neat name."

"Almost as good as Spooky," the man nodded.

Spooky shuddered. Their conversation was almost surreally normal. As normal as you could converse with a man holding a gun on you, that is. "So, what can I do for you, Ice Man?"

"Thank you for asking, Spooky," he said, polite derision dripping from his voice as he said her name. "I guess you can imagine the astronomical price our government, not to mention several others, would be willing to pay for someone like you?"

"You're planning on selling me to the highest bidder?" she asked, doing her best to look amused, but probably failing miserably. "You already have a buyer?"

"At the moment, no," he admitted. "No one would take me seriously without some form of proof."

"And how do you plan to get your proof?" she asked.

The Ice Man switched his gun to his left hand, and then pulled a thin electronic device out of his coat pocket. It was a Motorola phone, capable of filming a short video. "Funny thing, isn't it, Spooky? A regular cell phone and anyone can be a spy these days. So, if you'll be kind enough to jump?" he asked, moving closer to them with the gun.

Balcher blanched at the demand. The thought of Spooky jumping over the edge of the roof was crazy. This guy was out of his mind. There was no such thing as teleportation, not without some kind of futuristic machine or something.

Was there?

He had no choice; he'd have to take the guy down. And he couldn't get at his own gun fast enough; the guy would shoot him before he could get his jacket out of the way. He should have already had it handy. But he was so disoriented from all these extraneous images and feelings that he wasn't working on all cylinders at the moment. Even so, he couldn't let the guy toss Spooky off the roof, even if it cost him his own life.

He waited until the guy was barely three feet away, and then he jumped him. As big as he was, there was no finesse in the action. He threw his massive arms out, intent on knocking the gun from his hands, but the guy was too fast. Balcher saw the flash as the weapon fired. The bullet hit him square in the chest, and the blow was powerful enough to throw him backwards as the bullet tore through his body. The shock of the pain was immeasurable. As his world began to blur he remembered his premonition from the week before. Spooky was, indeed, going to be the death of him.

Spooky cried out as blood sprayed her face from the exit wound on Balcher's back. The sound of the gunshot was still ringing in her ears as he was thrown backwards by the blast. She grabbed hold of him, but his momentum pushed her towards the ledge and over it. She felt her feet leave the roof and the sensation of falling was all around her.

As she fell, her mind went into triple time as it plowed through the possibilities. Balcher was probably dead already, but if she left him behind to hit the ground she would never know for sure that she couldn't have saved him.

She wasn't sure she could trip with him either. Having barely recovered from her last trip, she probably didn't even have the strength to take herself out of there, much less him. But if she did trip and take him with her, what would happen? Her first thought was that they'd probably get lost forever in the lights. She wouldn't have the strength or the know-how to put them back together correctly.

You can do it!

What was that? She heard the voice in her mind and for a split-second, she almost recognized it.

To save Balcher, she'd have to tell. She's never told anyone but her mother about her ability to teleport. And if her mother, God help her, didn't have the capacity to handle something so extraordinary from her five year old daughter, then it stood to reason that nobody else would.

You have to tell!

The voice sounded so sure, but even if it didn't, she had no choice. With the ground speeding towards her, Spooky blindly held onto Balcher, and then, with all her might she screamed, "Outta here!"

The very second the words left her mouth, the colors swirled. She felt lightning explode around her and the energy of their two life forms meshed until they were one being slamming through the vortex of space and time. The journey felt timeless, as if it lasted for years, taking her through a lifetime of Balcher's memories from the day he was born until the second he was shot, but then she felt a tearing sensation and the sound of a pop as they were ripped apart from each other. The fantastic light show stopped, and the world went black.

Chapter Seven

Balcher hit the ground hard and it hurt nearly as bad as he thought it would. The pain ripped through him for about two seconds and then it let go of him.

Wait a minute.

Surely, a fall from thirty floors up was enough to kill him? He opened his eyes and realized that he was not an ugly wet spot on a steaming hot parking lot, but a fully formed—and naked—man lying next to a naked woman inside of what looked suspiciously like a bedroom.

Was he dead? Was this what came after?

He touched his chest where the bullet had hit him and there was no blood, no hole. It was as if it had never happened. He moved around, worried that he'd hurt like hell, but he felt remarkably well for someone who had just died.

The naked woman lying next to him came into focus. It was Spooky. He looked her body over—he was a virile male and could not help it—but was surprised by what he saw. She looked a lot healthier than he'd imagined she would look beneath her clothes. But it wasn't just that, her face was a bit fuller, not gaunt like it looked just moments ago. Maybe she was dead, too?

He nudged her, but she didn't move. She was cold, though, her skin like ice. He watched for a moment and she began to shake. When the shaking began to look like convulsions, he finally realized that they were both alive, but that something was definitely wrong.

She appeared to be suffering from hypothermia. He felt the cold coming from her in waves as if she were sheathed in ice. Like the last few days, but a thousand times stronger, images and emotions were popping into his head and he didn't know where they were coming from. This time, though, he knew it was imperative that he trust his instincts.

He grabbed her up off of the floor and looked frantically around for a way to get her warm. He spotted a partially open door on the other side of a bed and headed for it. It was a bathroom and it had a huge sauna bath installed inside it. He placed her inside the tub and turned the hot water on full force, and then he got in with her. He pulled her body against his, holding her protectively, their bodies touching skin to skin from her head to her toes. He rubbed her with chafing motions hoping desperately to calm the shaking down to an acceptable level. He was beginning to feel the cold, too. It was seeping into his bones painfully. He clenched his teeth to keep them from chattering.

All the while this was happening, he was trying to accept the fact that she had just teleported them away from the rooftop of that casino. And that somehow, in the midst of the trip, she had repaired the bullet hole in his chest. He felt thinner, too, and a quick glance down at his body told him that it was true. He didn't have an ounce of fat on him anywhere. He hadn't been this lean when he was at boot camp for the marines.

His hands massaged Spooky's back and then went down to cup her bottom and pull her closer against him. The water was rising fast around them, but she was still shivering.

It was going to be okay, he could feel it. The cold was letting go of him, degree by degree. He groaned as a shudder ran through his entire body and he felt the shudder echo though Spooky as well. Damn, but she felt good in his hands, not the sack-full of bones he'd felt a few days ago when he'd stopped her from falling. At that exact moment, he realized where some of the fat from his body had turned up.

The thought nearly paralyzed him. He pulled her away from him long enough to check to see if all the rest of his parts were still there. They were.

One of his parts in particular was more than prominent. He scowled. Of all the times to be horny, this was not one of them. Still, he decided that it was the excitement of the situation that was causing his body's reaction and not the fact that he had a beautifully-shaped, naked woman lying against him. And yes, maybe it was specifically *this* naked woman who was guaranteed to bring about this reaction.

The air around them was filling with steam. The water had risen to just below his breastbone and Spooky was completely submerged except for her head which was nestled against his chest. The warmth had finally reached him, taking over and heating up his blood.

Spooky had almost stopped shivering, as well. There was only the infrequent tremor to show that she was still in distress. She murmured something unintelligible, and then Balcher felt her arms move. She stretched them around his chest and pulled herself tight against him, as if she wanted to merge right into his skin. Before he realized what she was doing, she moved up his body for a moment and then came down onto his arousal, fitting herself snuggly around his engorged penis and gripping her thighs around his hips. They were now as close as two human beings could get.

At first, he didn't move as he was both shocked and ecstatic. The embrace sent sensations slamming through his body and for the briefest of moments, he remembered being one with her from before. It was during those few seconds as they were flying across the universe like sparks from a fire on a hot summer night.

He knew her. He remembered that now. He knew everything about her. Her childhood memories were as much a part of him as they were of her. Everything that had ever been done to her, every hurt, every accomplishment, everything. All of it.

He knew her.

The emotions rifled through his body, almost painfully, as he remembered. But at the same time they also put him at the mercy of the greatest sexual need he had every felt. He and Spooky were forever connected on so many levels, but right now, they were connected physically, and he could not have stopped himself if he had wanted to.

He grabbed onto her buttocks and pulled her slightly away from him and then he jerked her hard against him so that he could feel himself plunge within her. Pleasure knifed through him, but it was not enough. He wanted more, so much more. On some level, he realized that he was experiencing sensations from both of them at the same time. He felt the pleasure of his penis rubbing against the slick tightness inside her vagina, but he also swore that he could feel her vagina clench in response to his invasion. Unable to stop himself, he pressed into her over and over again, each time harder than the time before. The sensations were out of this world and he nearly laughed aloud at the images that thought conjured in his mind.

Maybe Spooky was out of this world, alien. He didn't know and he didn't care. She was everything he wanted to see, to feel, to smell, to touch. The sensations of plunging inside of her were incredible, like his penis was a lightning rod and she was the lightning. The build-up of electricity was phenomenal and he almost feared the culmination of this mind-shattering ride.

When it came, he nearly blacked out. The orgasm sent a jolt of electricity throughout his entire body and he felt it in every cell of his being. It lasted and lasted, pleasure so immense, it was almost painful to behold, and he convulsed with the rapture of it.

Many, many minutes later, when he came to himself, he reached up and turned off the water. If he wasn't careful, the incredible lassitude that was so resolutely coming over him might end up drowning the both of them.

Fighting sleepiness, he ran his fingers over her back. Her skin was no longer cold. It fact, it was burning up. Even so, she was still clutched tightly around him, holding him captive inside her body.

It felt right. It felt perfect. They were meant to be this way.

His rough hands continued to smooth their way over her back as he contemplated the last few extraordinary hours of his life. One thing was for certain. He was no longer the man he was three days ago. Hell, he was not even the same man he was three hours ago. Nothing was ever going to be the same again.

Chapter Eight

Spooky stretched languorously under the sheets. She didn't want to wake up; she'd never felt more comfortable in her life. If not for the little voice in the back of her mind telling her to open her eyes, she would have laid there for much longer.

But the little voice wouldn't be quiet. She opened her eyes and that's when she saw him.

Balcher sat sprawled in the big chair in the corner of her room with his legs propped up on the prim looking footstool she purchased at a yard sale only last week. His eyes were barely opened, but he became alert when he saw her move. He was covered half-way with a quilt which fell down around his waist when he sat up. Something about him looked different, but she was still too fuzzy to figure out what it was.

She was not surprised to see him there. Her dreams told her he would be. She sat up in the bed and realized that she was dressed, at least partially.

She switched on the bedside lamp. "How long have I been sleeping?" she asked, her hands straightening the t-shirt she was wearing. Something felt different. She looked down at herself and saw breasts under the shirt. She reached her fingers up and lightly touched the outside of the shirt, thinking that Balcher must have put her bra on, but there was no such constricting underwear anywhere in sight. It was all her.

"Well, I'll be damned," she muttered.

"I couldn't have said it better myself," he said, getting up from the chair, and after wrapping the quilt around him more snuggly, he came to stand beside her at the bed. He half expected her to pull away from him because the Spooky he knew from before, would have. When she didn't, he sat down onto the mattress beside her. "Do you remember anything that happened?"

She reached out and touched his back. She remembered the bullet exiting near his shoulder blade and how the blood sprayed her face. "You have no scar," she said wonderingly. Her fingers went down to his waist and she felt the indenture of the muscles there and finally noticed what was missing.

"Oh, my God!" she cried. Then she jumped up and ran to the bathroom.

Balcher ran after her wondering if something really bad had just happened, but he grinned when he saw what she was doing. She was on the scales and laughing like a hyena. In fact, the feeling of laughter hit him before he actually saw what she was doing, and somehow, he knew exactly what was going on in her head.

"How much did you gain?" he asked, smiling broadly.

"Twenty-two pounds!" she nearly screamed with glee. "I weigh a hundred and twenty-five pounds! I've never weighed that much," she said dancing around. She ran to the mirror—previously known as the torture device—and tore off her shirt to check out her reflection. "I have boobs!" She danced a little more and then laughed. "I jiggle!"

"You certainly do," he said admiringly.

She ran to him and threw her arms around him for a hug. "Thank you, so much," she said raggedly, her emotions finally catching up with her.

He felt her emotions pelt him and he knew that she was thanking him for so much more than the extra weight. In just a few hours, he had gotten to know this woman intimately and he suspected that she knew him just as thoroughly.

"It's like I've known you forever," he whispered, still holding her tightly.

She pulled back to look in his face. "I know. It's kind of scary, isn't it?" Then she took a step away from him and put her shirt back on. "You look good in a quilt."

"You're feeling the need to pull away from me," he said, catching a breath of a thought from her, and then held a hand up when her eyes darkened as if to hide what she was feeling. "I don't mean just physically. I know what's happened between us is scary, but it's also a good thing."

To Balcher, knowing somebody intimately—in this case, from right inside her own mind—*was* a good thing, even though Spooky may be having trouble with the idea. And because of what they'd been through, he realized that he knew just what to say to ease her misgivings.

He could never lie to her. If he could tell what she was feeling by just being close to her, then it was safe to say that she should be able to read him the same way. This 'open' communication between them could make for a difficult relationship if they weren't careful, and at some point, it might be conducive for them to find a way to close off their feelings, but he was grateful for it now.

She closed her eyes and took a deep breath. He could tell that his words affected her, calmed her a bit, and then he felt her touch his mind. It was almost a physical sensation. She opened her eyes and gazed at him soulfully. She believed him, he could feel it.

Even so, it was still overwhelming to her. She turned and walked into the bedroom to rummage through her clothes drawer in search of a pair of pants big enough to fit her now. She found a pair of sweat pants and pulled them on.

He followed her and watched as she dressed. "I guess you know what happened in the bathtub?" he asked, still guilty over his lack of control and the fact that she had been unconscious when it happened. It didn't matter that he'd felt her responses from inside her mind, or had he?

"I felt it, even though I was unconscious. And I think that I initiated it, so don't worry yourself about it," she admitted as she looked at him. Then she dodged the subject. "I'm sorry, but I don't have any men's clothes. I'll have to go out and buy you something to wear."

If she didn't want to talk about it, he wouldn't force her. He wasn't getting any fear from her, at least not the kind of fear a woman would feel towards a man that had just sexually assaulter her. No, the fear he felt from her came from the overwhelming need she felt inside of herself for him. He was glad for that information, but he didn't dare call her on it.

"Just drop me by my place—"

"Your old clothes won't fit," she said, eyeing his waistline as she brought a fingernail to her mouth in order to nervously chew on it. "I'd say you've dropped at least two sizes. You're what? A thirty-four waist with a thirty-eight inch length now?"

Her nervous habit touched him. "I guess," he said, turning to look at himself in the mirror as he stood next to her. "The thirty-eight length part is right. But it's been a while since I could get into a thirty-four inch waistline. I'm afraid I like chocolate bars too much."

Spooky laughed and then reached out and patted his tummy as if she couldn't resist the excuse to touch him. "Did you know that your candy bar addiction is the only thing I liked about you up until now? I'd get mad as a hornet sometimes when I'd think about you and then this image of you chomping on a Mars bar would come up and make me smile."

He put his hand over hers on his stomach. "I liked everything about you, Sarah," he said, using her real name purposely.

"Not everything," she corrected him as she pulled her hand out from under his. The physical connection was too strong and it seemed to cloud her mind. She picked up her brush from the dresser and began brushing her hair. "You thought I was too skinny and that I didn't dress well. And my crush on Davenport really pissed you off."

"If you knew what a piece of crap he was—"

She shrugged, the aggravation in his voice sending a thrill down her spine. It sounded like jealousy. If he was jealous, that meant he that he felt possessive of her. She liked that possibility because she'd never really belonged with anyone before. "I do know, now. Thanks to you. But he was good to me at a time when nobody else seemed to care about me. It was because of him that my life got changed around."

"If you'd come to anybody but him—"

"Nobody would have believed me," she finished for him. "Nor would they have needed my information so much that they would have used me to the point that Davenport has. If he hadn't used me, I would have never become a private detective. Regardless of his motives, it all turned out good for me." She shrugged again and then put her boisterous hair up into a pony tail. The look was so much better with her face filled out a little. And she noticed that her hair even looked healthier. She wondered what she could have taken from Balcher to get that?

"Don't worry about it," he said to her unspoken question. "I feel fine. As a matter of fact, I feel better than I ever have. Just hungry."

"You can read my mind," she stated, a mixture of wonder and horror appearing on her face as she turned to stare at him. Her mind had been so busy with everything that had happened, the trip, the lovemaking, that she hadn't caught on to the fact that she was hearing his thoughts, yet.

"Now, Sarah, don't get upset—"

"Spooky, call me Spooky. How did the thought come to you? Was it in words? Or was it like a picture, or a flash of emotion? Wait! Think of something...um...a question. Something out of the blue. I want to see if I can read your mind."

Balcher felt the panic coming from her. He had assumed that she could read minds from before, but maybe that wasn't the case. In his mind, he asked, *What do you want for breakfast?*

"What do I want for breakfast?" she gasped. "That's what you asked, wasn't it? Oh, my God! I've never picked up complete phrases before! Only visuals, emotions, abstract names, that kind of stuff. This is amazing!"

Then she looked like she was about to faint. She stumbled back to the side of the bed before her legs gave out and she sat down. "This is scary. That's what this is!"

Balcher sat down beside her and took her hand in his. "What's so scary about it? Because of the trip, we know each other inside out. What difference does it make if we can read each other's minds?"

She pulled her hand away. "I need to think. But not with you in here." She looked at him pleadingly. "Please, just go brush your teeth or something. I have an extra tooth brush in the cabinet. And then, if you want, you can check out my cabinets in the kitchen. They're well stocked. I eat like a horse."

Balcher could see that she needed the space and that there was no use trying to talk her out of it. It was another one of those things that he just *knew* about her. He reluctantly decided to give her the privacy she wanted.

He went to the bathroom. After using the toilet, he weighed himself on her scales. Naked, he weighed two hundred and twelve pounds. Wow! That was a forty-three pound loss! If she took twenty-two pounds from him, then where did the other twenty-one pounds go?

Then he remembered. The answer came floating into his head like a forgotten name he was trying to remember. She'd used them to fuel the trip, as she called it. His head started to hurt as he went in search of more answers. All of her memories were there; they were just tucked away, as if in books on a library shelf.

He moved to the mirror to get a better look at what he'd become, this time without the quilt wrapped around him. He almost couldn't believe what he was seeing. He was lean, almost to the point of gaunt. All he could see was the definition of muscles—thank God he'd stayed current with his workout at the gym—and in a few places, the hollows between bones, especially around the ribs. He turned and looked over his shoulder at his backside. Even there, there was little fat left. He had enough muscle to fill him out back there, thankfully, but not much else. All over his body, his skin was tight, following every line and indentation of his musculature and skeletal system.

It was a weight-loss wet dream, but it un-nerved him. He forced himself to take a closer look at his face. It was thin, but not too bad, and his cheekbones were more prominent. His previously-broken nose still looked a bit lop-sided and that made him smile because he liked his nose just the way it was. His brown eyes looked the same, his mouth, too. He pulled his lips away from his teeth and studied them. Something was different in there, but he couldn't put his finger on it, at first. Then it came to him. He had all his teeth—that molar at the top left that he had to have pulled a couple of years ago was back, big as life. He leaned into the mirror to look closer. Then he tapped it with his finger. Sure enough, it was real.

He pulled back from the mirror to check out the last thing on his list. He knew from the glimpse he'd had of himself in her bedroom mirror earlier that his hairline had drastically changed, and that wasn't the only thing.

He sighed. His hairline had been receding for the last couple of years. It wasn't much, certainly nothing he worried about. He even liked the way it made him look a little more intelligent. But that didn't matter now because it was back with a vengeance. Not only that, it was an inch longer than he regularly kept it and curly!

She had given him some of her hair.

My God! What else did she share with him?

The thought caused his heart to race. He knew his sexual equipment was right where it was supposed to be and in fine working order, but he couldn't help worrying about the rest of him.

And what about her? Did she take on damaged internal parts from that bullet that blew through his chest less than seventeen hours ago?

He searched his mind for answers, hoping to find them in her databanks—he preferred to think of them that way—and he came up empty. Besides, she wouldn't know the answer to that, would she? She's never teleported and brought anybody along with her before.

Maybe that's what she was in the bedroom obsessing over. He was thinking so loud to himself, about himself, that he couldn't hear her thoughts. He began the process of quieting his mind so that he could hear her, and then suddenly stopped himself.

She didn't want him in her head right now. She wanted to be alone. Peaking into her thoughts from another room was just as bad as eavesdropping.

He sighed in frustration and then tried imagining a wall around his mind, a fortress to close off his thoughts and feelings. With that wall in place, he found her extra toothbrush in its original un-opened packaging and used it to brush his teeth. Then, wrapping a towel around himself for modesty's sake, he headed for the kitchen.

He'd do this her way. They would eventually have to talk this out, but if he had to wait, then he could certainly do it and eat at the same time. He was starving!

Spooky was scared. She was scared to death. Balcher didn't know what he was in for. The Ice Man was not going to give up, she had no doubts about that. And if he had been able to catch their disappearing performance on video, then he'd have all the evidence he needed to sell her to the highest bidder. If she had only herself to worry about, it might not be such a bad situation. I mean, how in the world could anyone imagine that they could capture a woman who could teleport? And even if they could catch her, how would they keep her?

But the Ice Man, or Nicholas Brandson, which was likely an alias, would now have Balcher to hold over her head. If he got his hands on Balcher, she'd have no choice but to do anything he wanted her to do.

She squeezed her eyes shut. Balcher. Never in a million years would she have pictured him to be the man that he was. He was so gruff on the outside, but inside? He was one of the gentlest souls she'd ever known. And he was willing to give up his life for her. That became horribly obvious on that casino rooftop.

She realized now that he'd been attracted to her for a long time. Given the way he often treated her, that fact actually surprised her. She never felt an inkling of it during those years when they'd sparred practically every time they came into the same room with each other.

It was the touching that day at the precinct that did it. She thought back on that moment and realized that she had been more aware of him since then. She remembered pulling away from him in initial fear, but something had happened while he held her. Her soul had reached through and found him to be welcoming. She was so surprised to feel that from him that she touched him deeper than she's ever touched another human being. She couldn't have stopped herself if she'd tried.

The trip had fused them together in the most elemental way, but it was that first touching that brought them together. They both recognized something inside of each other that day, something that pulled them relentlessly towards each other.

It wouldn't have mattered if the Ice Man had never existed. They would have come together eventually.

Come together.

Her face heated as she remembered their time in the bathtub. Balcher was feeling guilty at what happened, but he shouldn't. She had wanted it with everything inside of her. Even unconscious, she had wound herself around him. She was too far gone to actually participate, but she was with him at every moment of their coupling. She'd felt the trembling need, the electric tingling, the wracking orgasms.

It was powerful stuff. And she wanted it again. She wanted it forever.

But she'd have to take care of the threat against Balcher and herself first.

Chapter Nine

"Smells good," Spooky said, leaning against the doorjamb inside the doorway to the kitchen.

"I'm an excellent cook," Balcher bragged, looking amazingly hot in the flimsy towel that surrounded his lean hips. He was whipping up an omelet and the aromas encircling the kitchen were mouth watering.

"Wow, a man after my own heart."

"I am after your heart, that's true. But I have to warn you, I'm after the rest of you, too," he said, reading her desire for him in her eyes. He was glad to see it there. He wasn't sure what she had been trying to talk herself out of back there in her bedroom, but it was a huge relief that making love with him wasn't a part of it.

She read that thought and smiled. "You're in big trouble, you know?"

"Really?" he asked with a raised eyebrow.

"Really," she stated. "I am a woman with huge appetites. It's going to be a difficult job satisfying me."

He snorted in laughter and then caught himself and coughed. It was remarkable how easy he felt with her, and she was beginning to feel it with him, too. It was as if they were an old married couple after a lifetime of loving together, except that the passion was fresh and amazing. "That was *so* over the top for you, Spooky. But I have to say, I like the imagery."

She made a face at him. "So, I'm not a femme fatale. But I wasn't lying about my appetite for food. You'll find that out when you watch me eat. It's something about my gifts and my metabolism, I guess."

Balcher moved the pan off of the hot eye and then headed across the room to take her in his arms. "You are a femme fatale. At least, you will always have me bamboozled."

He looked into her gray-blue eyes and really saw their beauty for the first time. Shadows, like pain, moved through their depths and he leaned close to kiss them away. The first touch of their first kiss was soft, like the brush of butterfly wings.

Then the touch of their lips moved beyond initial wariness and grew responsive, his tongue wetting her lips and then opening them to move inside. Tongues met and fire was unleashed, the conflagration between the two of them immediate, like a spark to a thousand matches. It burned them up, the need for each other consuming them to the extent of pushing everything else out of their heads. Nothing but the connection between them mattered.

Balcher's towel fell to the ground and he picked Spooky up and wrapped her legs around his waist. Then he marched her to the kitchen table and, pushing the plates he'd arranged so nicely on the table out of the way, he sat her down onto it.

He wrenched the old t-shirt over her head and pulled his mouth away from hers. He pressed his lips and tongue to the skin of her breasts, tasting her, and then taking her nipple into his mouth to suckle it. The sensation was wild. He felt his own nipples contracting as if she had her mouth on him, too. Again he felt the duality of their lovemaking, the feeling of taking and receiving at the same time.

Not taking his mouth from her breast, he reached down with one hand and grabbed the top of her sweatpants and panties. With his other arm, he held her off of the table slightly, just enough to yank her clothes over her buttocks and down her legs.

She kicked them off and again wrapped her legs around his hips, bringing the base of her legs into contact with his arousal.

Balcher heard her moans aloud, and in his head at the same time.

He sucked her breast harder before reaching down with one hand and rubbing his fingers between the folds of her sex. She writhed against him and he almost shattered.

It was amazing because he wasn't even inside her. Yet here he was, about to come by just pleasuring her.

"Inside me," she gasped. "Want you inside me."

He barely heard her words, but he didn't have to, they were in his head. He removed his hand and then placed the head of his penis at her opening. Before he pressed into her, he brought his face up close to hers. He wanted to see her eyes when he entered her.

As their gazes locked, he pressed himself inside her. Her eyes darkened as she took him in, surrounding him with her blazing wetness. Breathtaking pleasure assaulted him, doubling in on him again, and he pounded into her.

Spooky felt the swirling sensations reverberating through the nerves of her skin, her bones, her womb. Like before, she felt everything he was feeling, the pleasure overlapping her own chaotic tremors. Were mere human beings supposed to feel this much?

The pleasure mounted until Spooky actually heard a scream come from her own lips. Clenching her teeth, she splintered, she crashed, she burned and burned and burned.

She gasped for breath, but she was not the only one. Balcher collapsed onto her, pinning her to the table, heaving as he tried to regain his breath. She pushed him off of her. She had to. She couldn't breathe.

She stumbled a short distance away and nearly fell into one of her kitchen chairs. She dropped her head between her knees and breathed deeply, trying to keep from passing out. What a rush!

Eventually, she raised her head and watched him as he pushed himself away from the table and managed to find a seat in a chair on the other side of the table.

"I think..." He stopped to catch his breath again. "I think, the next time we do that, we need to find a bed." He sat there for about a minute and then he pushed himself out of the chair and went to the refrigerator. He opened the door and brought out a carton of orange juice. Grabbing a couple of glasses from the cupboard, he poured them both full, and then handed a glass to her before downing his own in one long gulp.

He refilled his glass and then went to the stove and divided the omelet up between two plates and brought them to the table. He found a couple of forks that hadn't hit the floor during the desperation of their lovemaking a few moments ago, and slid one of them towards her.

"Eat up," he growled, his voice still gruff from exertion.

Spooky watched it all in amazement. She was still numb from the sex. With her nerve endings tingling, she tried to reach for the juice, but her hand would not obey. Balcher must have some kind of constitution to be able to move so quickly after what just happened between them.

She found her voice. "Is it going to be like that every time?"

Balcher looked up from his plate. "I don't know. It might wear down after a while, like regular sex amongst married couples does. But then again, it might not." His eyes narrowed. "Are you starting to second guess it, uh, what's happening between us?"

Spooky shook her head. "No. Just wondering. I might have to start taking more vitamins, though."

Balcher coughed to squelch a laugh. "You and me both, sweetheart."

She was finally able to move her arms, so she picked up her glass and tasted the fresh orange juice, the cold wetness of the juice quenching the dryness of her mouth. She watched him eat and couldn't help wondering if he had been changed by their connection to the point where he'd spend the rest of his life in a constant state of starvation like she did. She also couldn't help wondering if he felt the same thing she did when they were making love. If he felt the giving and the receiving at the same time.

"I felt it," he said, looking up at her. "I felt everything I did to you as if it was being done to me. Talk about perfect sex. When I give to you, I give to myself, and visa versa."

He'd read her mind again. Funny, she didn't mind it as much this time. She also liked what he said about perfect sex and couldn't wait to test the theory on him. She looked across the tabletop at his stomach and her eyes followed the line of hair down his body until it disappeared behind the table. She licked her lips.

"Oh, no, you don't. Not now. I don't think I'd live through it," Balcher chuckled. Then he scowled at her grin. "Eat your omelet," he ordered.

Spooky chuckled as she picked up her fork and tackled her food. She found the omelet quite good, actually. Better than in any restaurant around here, for sure. Besides, she needed the sustenance. Especially for what she had in mind for Balcher later.

If there was a later.

She frowned. They really needed to know what was going on in the outside world. If she was right, the Ice Man would have gone down to the parking lot and looked for her clothes, Balcher's too, hoping for more clues as to who they were. If he got to them before they were found by anyone else, he would have Balcher's wallet and I.D.

It was all a matter of time. If he did have possession of Balcher's wallet, then things were going to come to a head pretty fast. If not, then they might have a few days to get ready for the guy.

"You think I should call the station and see if anybody turned my stuff in?"

Again with the mind reading! She sighed, but she guessed it saved time. And it might come in handy later.

"Yeah. Check with Zack and see if he knows anything. Tell him whatever you think he'll believe to keep things from blowing up on you at the station. If I were you, I'd think about using some vacation time, too. I don't see how we can go to Davenport with this kind of trouble."

Balcher grunted at the sound of Davenport's name. Then he finished the last bite of his omelet and put his dishes in the sink before heading to the living room to make his call.

Spooky heard him talking, his voice rising slightly in irritation like it always seemed to do when he was conversing with Zack. Those two made a strange pair, but they were comfortable with each other.

Her stomach rumbled, taking her mind off of Balcher, and she stuck her fork into another bite of the omelet. Then something about the way her arm looked caught her attention. She stared at it mesmerized, twisting it slowly back and forth. Funny, she could swear that there was more muscle mass there.

She glanced down at her thighs, still naked from the impromptu lovemaking. She touched them, running her hands along the lean lines of muscle that was newly formed there, making her way down to her calves. She wasn't overtly muscular, but she was certainly well defined.

Balcher walked back into the kitchen, looking at her strangely. "Those muscles weren't so well formed before, were they?"

She looked up at him and numbly shook her head. "No. I mean, there was a little muscle, but nothing like this. I don't work out much. I've always been afraid to. Because of my metabolism, you know. I needed every calorie I could ingest to keep my strength up. I couldn't afford to waste it on exercise."

He frowned. "I know what you're worried about, but you're wrong. You didn't take any of that from me. I checked myself out in the mirror thoroughly this morning. Everything's intact." He moved to the table and sat down across from her—their sexual chemistry was too combustible for him to chance holding her close to him at this moment—and then reached out for her hand.

She placed her hand in his showing her trust, or maybe it was her fear. "Then how did this happen?" she asked shakily.

He pulled from her memories, gaining impressions of the theories she'd come up with over the years to explain her abilities. They were slightly clouded already, and he realized that in the hours, days, and weeks to come, that they would probably fade a lot more. He was actually grateful for that. Merging with Spooky had been the most intimate experience of his life, but the allusion of being two people at once, one female, the other male, was difficult to cope with. Knowing that those blurred lines would slowly begin to right themselves, was comforting.

"Going on previous assumptions," he began, and then he corrected himself. "*Your* previous assumptions seem to indicate that whenever you had to remake yourself after a trip, you used the only pattern you had available to you. Your own DNA footprint, so to speak. But this time, when you had me with you, you had an entirely different pattern to work with."

"I think I see what you're getting at," she murmured. "I don't know how I can break down matter and change it into energy and then reverse the process miles away at a different location, but I've been doing it since I was five years old."

Balcher didn't see a flinch on Spooky's face, but he felt one in her head. It was a quick flash of her as a five year old child being molested by her mother's boyfriend. The act traumatized her so badly; her unique mind found a way out of the horror and took her to a safe place.

"You saw that, didn't you?" she asked.

He nodded. "I guess, but I already knew about it. Your memories are all there, especially the stronger ones like this one, but they're jam-packed into my head like a stack of files a mile high. It's been difficult sorting through them."

"I've had the same trouble with yours," she admitted. "But when I say something to you that jogs an old memory, I can see your memory as plain as if I was there myself." She pulled her hands out of his. "But you don't think this will always be the case, do you?"

He leaned back in his chair and watched her as she got up and gathered her strewn clothes. She put them on and then sat back down to continue their conversation, but not before she threw him his towel.

He felt her defenses come up to shield her heart. The act of putting on clothes was just an outward manifestation of her inner fears. In deference to her feelings, he placed the towel she tossed him over his lap before answering. "No, I can already feel your memories fading. But I need you to understand something. It's only logical that it should be this way. That memory when you were five was horrifying, but it's been overshadowed by years of living now. You couldn't survive on a daily basis if that memory remained in your head as fresh as the day it happened."

He leaned forward earnestly. "Spooky, I don't think we'll ever forget each other's memories completely. They'll just fade comfortably away and we'll be left with the feeling that we've known each other for our whole lives."

"And that's comforting to you, isn't it."

"Sure it is, but please don't take my comfort as meaning I don't want you close. I do. I guess, it's more my male pride speaking." He leaned closer and his brown eyes twinkled devilishly. "You may not know this about me, but I've always been kind of macho."

His teasing warmed her from the inside. "No, you don't say?" she said, rolling her eyes.

He laughed, "It's true. So can you imagine how it feels for me to know exactly what it feels like being female...being *you*. There were instances last night that I almost couldn't remember if I was me, or if I was you. So yes, I hope that fades. We are two separate human beings. Maybe we do know each other better than anybody else will ever know us, and maybe we'll always be able to read each other's minds, but I like who I am and I like who you are. And I'm not sure we could survive connected to the extent that we're connected right now."

"Okay, that makes sense," she agreed, nodding.

Feeling like he was on safer ground, Balcher went on. "Getting back to what happened when we tripped, I think that your mind found some of my...um...patterns preferable to the ones it had used before. Maybe that's where those missing twenty-one pounds went. Your brain chose to remake that fat into muscle."

She shook her head. "I don't think so. Trippin' always took several pounds off of me. I lost seven pounds the other day after I tripped out of the Radicom office. So, it makes sense that it would take twenty or more pounds to carry us both through the lights."

"That might have been true then, but you're physically stronger now," he stated.

She frowned. "What do you mean?"

"Think of a trained athlete, a man or a woman running a twenty-six mile marathon. For months, maybe even years, they've built themselves up to the task. The day of the marathon, they eat a high-carb breakfast and drink plenty of fluids and then they hit the pavement. Is it difficult for them? Hell, yeah! But they get through it, and that evening they go out and celebrate.

"Now, consider some regular guy that sits at a desk for eight hours a day. His only exercise is when he walks to the mailbox and back. Let's say this dude decides for some cockeyed reason to get up and participate in that marathon. He's nearly dead a mile down the road, his heart is racing and he can hardly breathe, and you can bet he won't be going out to celebrate that night. He probably won't even make it to work for the rest of the week."

"I guess I understand your analogy, but you're forgetting that I was used to tripping...and the visions, too. All of that was normal for me."

"Normal, yes, but you didn't train for them properly."

"I did—"

"Spooky, honey, you know I'm right. You have my knowledge base to compare with your own now. Proper nutrition and physical training can make a vast difference in how your body reacts to the trips, and the visions as well. Not to mention that you've depended on them far too much over the years and—"

"For somebody who munches out on candy bars like they're going out of style, you sure do have a lot of opinions," she grumbled, pulling back and crossing her arms across her chest.

He chuckled and leaned back himself. "That's the downside of this thing of ours. We know each other's faults as well as our strengths. But that doesn't make me wrong. I've lived a rough thirty-four years—eight of them in the Marines—depending on nothing but my smarts and my brawn. My combat training makes my body a dangerous weapon. I can take down a man much bigger than me in seconds flat. I know how to use other weapons, too; guns, knives. Those are useful forms of self-protection for someone in the law enforcement field.

"And," he continued before she could say something to refute him, "If you'd had a gun on you that night at the Radicom office and the expertise to use it, you might not have had to trip out of there."

Spooky hated it, but he was right. With the extra weight and the musculature, she felt better than she'd ever felt in her life. She didn't even feel the flu-like sickness she usually felt after a trip. She felt strong, capable. And he was right about something else, too. She had depended too much on her abilities. She used them almost exclusively in her work.

All this time and she never realized that she was that weak woman trying to run that marathon. She'd been doing it her whole life.

Balcher leaned forward again. "It's not too late. After we take care of the Ice Man, we'll set up a regimen of weight training and karate classes. You should already have access to most of that stuff in your head, if you check out my databanks."

"Your databanks, huh?" she said with a smirk.

"That's the only way I can keep all this stuff straight. Giving it a name makes it feel more natural. It's better than saying yours, mine and ours."

She nodded. "You really haven't said much about how you feel about all of this. I mean, we haven't touched on some of the major stuff."

His left eyebrow went up. "Really? Like what?"

"Like the fact that you've suddenly become psychic and God knows what else," she said. "I didn't just change your physique when we tripped; I messed with your brain chemistry."

He shrugged. "Actually, that started before we tripped. Something happened that day at the police station. I didn't realize it at first, but there were a few weird instances when I knew some things without knowing how I knew them. It was disconcerting, for sure."

Her shoulders drooped. "I thought that maybe it had. I touched your mind that day, but I didn't realize that I left something behind."

She suddenly sat up straight.

"Oh, my God! What if I've been doing that all along? All those people I've touched over the years! What if I changed them, too?" Her heart was beating double time and she jumped up out of the kitchen chair and marched into the living room. Part of her wanted to run screaming from the house in horror.

Balcher tucked the towel in at his waist and ran after her. "Don't panic. We'll figure it out. You didn't do anything on purpose, honey, so don't go blaming yourself until we know for sure what's happened."

"That woman at the police station," she said, breathing hard. "We can start with her." She paced the length of the living room, back and forth. "Oh, God, I can't believe it! She was an evil woman and she'll use the gift to hurt people. I know it."

"Look, your getting upset is not helping. You're borrowing trouble, and we already have enough of that. What we need is a game plan," Balcher said, taking her hands in his and leading her to the couch to sit down. "First, I need clothes. You'll have to go out and get them for me. But until we know if the Ice Man has my wallet, we can't chance going by my apartment."

"What'd Zack say when you spoke to him?" she asked, her hands nervously twisting in his. All this energy. She didn't know what to do with it. She pulled her hands out of his and jumped up to start pacing again.

Balcher's eyes followed her. "He's gonna head by the casino and look for my wallet at their lost and found. Casinos are good about stuff like that. I told him that I must have dropped it when I was following you. I also told him that I caught whatever it was you had the other day, and that I wouldn't be coming back to work for a few days."

"Wow, you're good. None of that was technically a lie," she murmured, still pacing. For a person who was usually exhausted most of the time, this excess energy was thing to behold.

He grunted. "Sticking close to the truth is always best. And it won't hurt him as much later when he sees me and wonders what the hell happened to me."

"Well, the sick story will help with the weight loss, but you'll have to find a barber and get that buzz cut your so fond of, or he's gonna think you went in for a hair transplant."

"Yeah, that's just so funny," he grated as she paced by him for the tenth time. He jumped up off the couch, her restlessness catching on and making him jumpy. "What possessed you to give me all this hair in the first place?"

She stopped in front of him. "Oh, are we feeling insecure all of a sudden?" she said with a raised eyebrow. "Never mind," she said guiltily. "I don't think I did it because of you. I think I just wanted my own hair thinner." She resumed pacing.

He frowned. "Well, it's actually good that you did. I'm forty-three pounds lighter and I have a lot of hair now in the place of my buzz cut. It's a perfect disguise, or at least as good a one as I can get without camouflaging my height. And your whole body shape has changed."

He studied her for a moment. "While you're out this afternoon, grab a hair color. Red, maybe. That'll change your appearance enough to make you unrecognizable as well."

She nodded. "Okay, so the plan is to go out and buy you a wardrobe—"

"Not a whole wardrobe, Spooky. A few shirts and a couple of pairs of pants will do me for a week or so. Without my wallet, I don't have access to my checking account or credit cards."

"You don't need them. I'll buy your clothes."

"I don't need you to buy all of them. Just enough to get me by," he said, frowning.

"As you pointed out, Balcher, you've dropped forty-three pounds. You'll need a wardrobe eventually. And so will I, obviously. I may as well get everything while I'm out."

"That could get pretty expensive, Spooky," he said catching hold of her arm as she went by him again, forcing her to be still for a moment. At this pace, she was going to lose some of that precious weight she was so happy about.

At his touch, she finally realized what he was in a twit about. His male pride didn't like the idea of her paying for his clothes. Unfortunately, there was nothing she could do about that. She had funds, he did not. "Don't worry about the money. Being psychic is lucrative," she said, shrugging self-depreciatingly. "I've made over five hundred thousand dollars a year at the casinos alone. They all have me on speed-dial."

Balcher flinched. Not just at her casual mention of money, but at the memory—her memory—those words just sparked inside him. "You're not kidding, are you?" He frowned, and then he gave a searching look around the living room. After a moment he got up and walked over to the fireplace and knelt down at the left side of the brick enclosure. He removed a brick at the base, and then another one, and then reached his hand into the hole. He pulled out a wad of cash, all hundreds, and it was only a small portion of what she had stashed in there.

He was nearly speechless, but somehow he managed to push out the words in his head. "You also have an off-shore bank account with close to a million dollars in it, as well as a couple of healthy banks accounts here in the city, don't you?"

She nodded affirmatively. "Desperate people are willing to pay a lot of money to find out things. I'm good at finding out things," she looked down at her feet, as if embarrassed by what she was saying.

Then, she realized that he knew what she was feeling and so she held her head up, tossing her wild hair back away from her face as she continued. "When I first started, I was charging the casino managers a thousand dollars a pop to tell them if they had any card-counters, pick-pockets, or flim-flam artists working their casinos. When they saw how good I was at it, they passed my name along to all the other hotels and casinos. Before long, I didn't have time to do anything but go from one casino to the next. I pushed my price up to ten thousand dollars a job and they didn't even blink. The work just kept piling in. When I went up to twenty grand, about half of the casino work came to a halt. I guess I finally priced myself out of the game. They only call me now if they've got a really hard case. That's what Harrell was arguing with me about yesterday when Zack had his adventure with the monkeys. He hates paying me that much, but he does it anyway if it'll save him some money in the long run." She glanced at Balcher after her long spiel. He seemed awed by the information. She could practically see the images in his head as he remembered all of this with her.

She shrugged. "For the last six months or so, I've had time to try my hand at more challenging work. I still take missing persons cases, here and there, and I don't charge those poor people much to work on them. I suppose I do it out of the need to feel honorable," she admitted. "So, as you can see, a few clothes aren't going to break me."

He eyed her carefully. "If you wanted to, you could take all of this money and disappear. That Ice Man character would never find you."

"You really think he would give up on an opportunity of a lifetime?" she asked with a disgusted snort. "Somebody like me is worth a fortune to him. He'll have that video he took documented as legitimate, and then he'll put my life on the auction block for every government agency willing to pay his price."

Balcher raised his hands as if to say 'give me a break.' "Well, then, beat him to the punch. Go to the pentagon and show them your stuff. They'll protect you."

Spooky was becoming frustrated at his refusal to see the truth. "Balcher, you're not thinking this through. Our government is no better than any of the rest of them. Do you actually think that they'll care about me? Their only concern will be to figure out how I do what I do, and then to try to duplicate it. I'll be a science experiment at worst, a government puppet or slave at best. I'd never have a choice in how I want to spend my life. And, if I did try to get away from them? They'd rather have me dead then chance me falling into the hands of another government."

Balcher didn't like her words. He'd given eight years of his life for his country and he would do it again, but she had a point. Her life would no longer be her own. He, certainly, would not be allowed to be a part of it.

"I love this country, too," she said, reading his mind. "I wouldn't want to live anywhere else. And if push came to shove, I'd work for our government before anyone else's. But you have to admit, this teleporting thing is irresistible. Scientists would be foaming at the mouth to get their hands on me. Especially, if they knew I could pass on the ability at will."

That last thought stunned him. "Pass it on? You think I could teleport on my own?" he asked hoarsely.

She shrugged. "I don't know what you can do. You've already demonstrated that you can read my mind. And you said something about being able to pick up information out of the air, so to speak, even before we tripped. Maybe, you should try picking up an inanimate object and see if you get visions from it. If you can do that, then it's not outside the realm of possibility that you can teleport, too, or even something more extraordinary, come to think about it. What says you have to be exactly like me? I may have re-wired your brain, but even I don't know exactly what I did to you."

She was a little troubled at the way he was taking the information. Maybe, he really hadn't thought all this through. Maybe, he was okay with a little mind reading and the super-sonic sex, but that was as far as he thought it should go.

She went to the hole in the brick fireplace and grabbed enough money to get her through the afternoon and then picked up her phone to call her favorite cab company for a ride.

She turned as she was about to walk out the front door. "We don't need to waste any more time today. I'll get whatever clothes I think we need and anything else I can think of that might come in handy if we have to go on the run. You stay here and give all this some thought. I've had a lifetime to get used to all this. It's only fair that you have a few hours to think about it."

She walked outside and sat in a chair on her porch to wait on the cab. As much as she wanted to, she couldn't help Balcher through this. He had some decisions to make and she couldn't be a part of that.

In the next few days, they'd have to work together to find the Ice Man and silence him. The exact meaning of that was not something Spooky wanted to contemplate. It was his survival verses hers...and Balcher's. One of the things that worried her most was what this final insult would do to a man of Balcher's character. He was not a murderer. But then, neither was she.

She was, however, a fighter. And she was more than willing to fight the Ice Man to the end.

Balcher heard her thoughts, even from inside the house. She might want her privacy, but he was going to do exactly what she told him to do; practice his abilities. He would follow her with his mind the whole time she was gone. He wanted to find out how far this mind reading thing would go.

One thing she certainly wouldn't have to worry about; he could kill the Ice Man without giving it a second thought. After all, the man had already killed him once, hadn't he? Just a little pay back. Simple as that.

He was beginning to look forward to it.

Chapter Ten

Spooky paid the cab driver as he dropped her off at the Treasure Island Casino. Balcher might not like this, but she had to know for sure if touching a person and gathering information from them could have altered them the same way it did Balcher. Of course, in seeing this particular client, she was metaphorically killing two birds with one stone.

She meandered through the crowd on the casino's gaming floor and then headed towards the elevators where she chose the floor that housed the casino's spa and beauty parlor. She was looking for Jenna Smith, a client of hers from three months ago. She'd found Jenna's missing husband, Terry, at a hotel in Reno with a big-busted brunette who, unfortunately, had more money than sense and believed the good looking devil when he told her he was not married. They'd been shacked up for three weeks and poor Jenna was left behind in Vegas terrified that her precious Terry had been kidnapped or something worse.

Jenna had been so grateful that Spooky had agreed to take her case, she had grabbed onto Spooky and held on as she cried her heart out. For Spooky, the contact had been painful, not to mention totally unnecessary because she had already gotten the rascal's whereabouts by sitting in his favorite easy chair when she came into the couple's house.

She hated it when people touched her uninvited, mostly because she hated invading their privacy. Some of the things she saw in people's minds were intensely private and should never be shared with anyone else. Things like their sexual habits—Spooky had seen more sex in her visions than the hardiest of porn fans—and she'd seen their fears and their self-hatreds, too. All things she considered herself better off not knowing.

But Jenna needed comfort that day and Spooky gave it to her, holding her longer than she normally would and trying her best to console her. Especially since she knew her findings were going to break that sweet little girl's heart.

Now, as she entered the spa area, Spooky was hoping that three months was long enough for Jenna to get over that cad she'd married. And, if Jenna had time today, she was also hoping to get the woman to color, cut, and style her hair. Jenna was the Treasure Island casino's premiere hair stylist.

She signed in at the desk and asked for Jenna, and then sat in the waiting room with a magazine to wait. She felt the wisp of a touch in her mind and jerked her head up.

Where are you?

Dang it! It was Balcher. *At the beauty parlor*, she shouted in her mind.

Okay.

Wow! It was as easy as that. Better than a cell phone. She rolled her eyes. It was just like him to want to know where she was every second. She brushed off the frustration. It was actually good to know that they could communicate at a distance. It wasn't the easy reading of the mind like when they were in the same room, but it was sufficient.

"Spooky!"

Spooky looked up in time to see Jenna coming at her for a hug. She stood up and managed to put the magazine between them so that the embrace was not as solid. She still got a flash. It was a sensation of someone that was genuinely happy. Spooky felt better about being here now. Besides, she would have to get used to Jenna's touch since she was actually considering letting Jenna do her hair.

They exchanged pleasantries and then Spooky cleared her throat. "I was wondering if I could get you to do something with this mess of hair," she said, pushing the curly mass away from her face. "And, I was thinking of going red."

"That would be so cool," Jenna enthused. "I'll make time for you, Spooky, don't you worry about that. Come on back."

Spooky followed the beautician back behind the wall that separated the quiet entrance way from the busy area beyond. Back there, she saw things that she'd never seen before in person. A couple of the women looked like aliens in a 60s B movie with their hair sticking out on what looked like silver shingles loaded down with white cake icing. Others sat beneath blowers with rollers bigger than Spooky's fist lining their heads in rows. There were women getting manicures and pedicures, and some really good looking hunks were massaging their calves, ankles, forearms and hands.

She felt like she was in the twilight zone.

"Over here, hon," Jenna said, pointing to a strange looking swivel chair.

Spooky sat down and was immediately covered with a pink plastic sheet. Then Jenna was forcing some kind of wire brush through her hair and nearly pulling her head off.

"You don't know how bad I wanted to do this the last time I saw you, Spooky," Jenna said, her hands moving so quickly that Spooky didn't have time to get much from the contact. "You have great hair, it just needs a good cut and some highlights. Besides wanting it red, do you have anything in mind or will you leave it up to me?"

Spooky was almost afraid to move. Jenna was tilting her head this way and that way so forcefully that she was compelled to just go along for the ride. "Uh...whatever you think," she murmured.

"Good," the girl said with satisfaction. "I see that you've put on some weight since the last time I saw you. With most women, I wouldn't dare bring that up, but it looks great on you."

"Yeah, I like it, too," Spooky said. She watched as Jenna mixed a concoction up in a bowl. It looked purple. Was that going on her hair? Apparently so. That and the other bowl of what she'd heretofore believed was cake frosting. Jenna lined up a stack of the silver shingles and then turned to Spooky with anticipation. Spooky almost winced as the woman took a paint brush and slathered some of the goop onto her head.

Hair styling aside, Spooky was getting perplexed about the fact that she was getting very little from her physical contact with Jenna. Maybe the girl was so caught up in her work that she wasn't putting anything else out there. She guessed she would have to get the information she came for in a different way.

"I was wondering how you were doing since the last time I saw you, Jenna. I mean, I know that was a terrible situation for you and I hated having to be a part of that," Spooky said in an effort to concentrate on her second reason for being here. It was difficult to do as she was becoming mesmerized by her own image in the mirror. Jenna's nimble fingers were manipulating strands of her hair, coating one lock with the frosting and wrapping it up in the silver and then coating the next in the purple goop.

Without a hitch in her pace, Jenna replied, "Oh, don't you worry yourself about any of that, Spooky. You don't know how much you helped me that day. I mean, there I was feeling like my life was crashing in on me and then, somehow, you're being there and comforting me made me feel better."

"Really? I'm glad I helped. So, anything exciting and new going on in your life?" Spooky felt like she was failing miserably with the questions. No wonder she was so dependent on her psychic abilities, she probably couldn't find the nose on her face without them.

"I've got a new guy." Jenna giggled. "Steven. He's really something, too. Not good looking the way Terry was, but he's a good man. I felt it the first time I saw him."

"You felt it?" Spooky asked shakily.

"Yeah. It was strange. I met him when he worked on my car six weeks ago and some inner voice just told me that I could trust him. That kind of thing's been going on a lot over the last couple of months. I'm getting better at my work, too. Everybody I've worked on lately tells me how good I've styled their hair. They say it's like I read their minds or something."

Spooky swallowed hard. "Are you psychic?" She tried to ask the question with a laugh, but it didn't come out all that well.

"No way." Jenna laughed. "I'm just more confident in what I do, I guess. Terry was a real downer, making me doubt myself all the time.

Since he's been gone, everything just seems to be falling in place."

"So you don't get...uh...feelings or visions when you touch something?"

"No, but wouldn't that be cool? My uncle Roy was psychic, or so my mama says. I've never met him, so I don't know for sure. How short do you want to go?" Jenna asked and then answered the question herself before Spooky could get her mind around the change of subject. "I think...a little past shoulder length. Yeah, that'd be perfect."

"Whatever you say," Spooky said timidly. The purple stuff and silver shingles was practically covering her head now.

Jenna wrapped a plastic bag around her head and then pointed her in the direction of a dryer. The girl flipped a switch on the device and then scurried off to do something else for another customer.

Spooky sat there with that dryer heating her head up and she could hardly think for the overwhelming fear that was clogging her mind. She had changed Jenna. It wasn't anything near the level of the changes she performed inside of Balcher's head, but it was there nevertheless.

Who else had she affected this way? God only knows.

Two hours later, she left the beauty parlor with an arm full of beauty products for her new hair style. It was actually a wonderful style and the color and highlights were fantastic, too. Nowhere near purple.

She hailed a cab and gave the driver the address of the closest mall. She spent five hours at the place: one hour at a big and tall men's store, three hours shopping for her own clothes and another hour in a shoe store. It was the first time in her life that she actually looked good in the clothes she was trying on and she found the experience totally engrossing.

She hit a grocery store on the way home and it was nearly seven o'clock in the evening when she came through her front door.

Balcher couldn't help her get any of the bags in because he was still naked except for the towel. He waited in the bedroom until the cab driver left and then walked into the living room and came to a dead stop.

He said, "You're beautiful." Her hair was the most gorgeous color of chestnut and the long layered cut and style was perfect for her face. Her clothes were fashionable, even to his untrained eye, and she wore them with more confidence than he'd ever seen Spooky possess before. If he hadn't been here for the transformation, he wouldn't have recognized her if he'd passed her on the street.

"Sorry I'm so late, I—"

"I know. I followed you the whole day."

"You what?" she asked.

"Well, I didn't actually follow you. But I kept an eye on you, so to speak. Every once in a while I'd check in to make sure everything was okay and when I saw what you were doing—"

"You saw me?" she asked, dumbfounded.

"Just a figure of speech. It was more like the hum of a television that is on but that you're not watching. You can hear what's going on, maybe get a glimpse of the action, more or less, but it's just kind of going on at the edge of your consciousness."

He saw that his words, not to mention his staring, was making her uncomfortable so he went over to the sofa to look through some of the packages labeled *Big and Tall*. He found a package of underwear. "Colored underwear?" he asked with a chuckle, ripping the package open. They were the kind that Michael Jordan hawked in those commercials of his. He pulled the navy blue pair on and dropped the towel.

They looked so cute on his tight, well-formed butt that Spooky wanted to pinch him.

"Don't even think about it," he grunted, not turning around. He found a pair of jeans and pulled them out to look at them. "Stretch jeans? Those are for sissies."

"Don't knock 'em until you try 'em," she said, rolling her eyes.

Balcher pulled the jeans on. Then he did a deep knee bend and jumped back up. "Hey, these are nice."

Spooky knew he'd like them. She bought the feminine version of them for herself after she tried them on and saw how they felt. Knowing the possibility that the both of them might drop weight suddenly was her reasoning behind the purchase. The jeans fit Balcher snuggly now, but they would still be okay if he lost weight or even if he gained a few pounds. Besides, she couldn't see the difference; they looked every bit as good as regular jeans.

"I got you three pairs of them in different colors. And some t-shirts for around here and some casual dress shirts for going out. There are a couple of silk shirts and matching ties to go with those suits," she said, pointing to the suit bags she laid over the back of the chair. Then she pointed to some boxes on the floor. "Those boxes are shoes, a pair of tennis shoes, a pair of loafers and a pair of black dress shoes and several pairs of socks of assorted colors. And in that green bag over there, you'll find a razor, some aftershave and shaving lotion, deodorant, another toothbrush and a comb. I couldn't think of what else to get for you."

He looked at her with appreciation. "This will be more than enough."

"So, you're no longer ticked off about me buying you clothes, I guess?" she asked dryly, watching him tie the laces of his gold trimmed black tennis shoes.

"Not since I remembered how rich you are," he said smugly, taking a royal blue t-shirt out of a bag and then pulling it over his head and smoothing it around his waist.

Man, he looked good! Blue was definitely his color.

Then Spooky's stomach growled and she just that moment recognized the smell in the air. "You made steaks?" she asked, running to the kitchen. She looked around the room, but there was nothing on the stove and nothing on the table, either.

"Sorry. I got hungry," he admitted sheepishly after following her into the kitchen. When she whirled around on him with a surprised look on her face, he held his arm up in defense and offered, "I've ordered a couple of pizzas. They'll be here in fifteen minutes."

"That is so...so wrong," she said with a flabbergasted shake of her head. Then she went passed him into the living room to grab up her bags and take them to her bedroom.

He followed her again. "Where do you want me to put my stuff," Balcher asked, amused as he stood in her bedroom doorway and watched her manhandle her new clothes. Boy! She was really mad. Lesson number one; don't fool around with Spooky's food!

"I have a guest bedroom you can use while you're here," she said. She threw the new sexy underwear she bought into her underwear drawer and slammed it.

"You really have a temper, don't you?" he asked.

"Ask me that the next time I eat all the food and leave you starving!" she growled.

His hands went up in surrender. "Okay, so I knew it was wrong when I did it. That's why I ordered the pizzas. You're going to have to cut me a break, here. I'm not good at handling these overwhelming appetites, yet."

Spooky's jerky motions stilled a bit. If anything, she understood the power of those hungers he mentioned. She supposed it would be difficult for someone who was not used to it. "It's simple," she murmured, turning to face him with a despondent look on her face. "When you plan a meal, make twice what you think you could possibly eat and you might come close to what you'll need. Double it, if I'm going to be sharing your meal."

She looked him over. "You don't have any reserves stored up in your body right now. Hunger will feel like it's gnawing on your backbone with these great big teeth. It can actually be painful, at times. Keep food with you at all times because you'll never know when the hunger pains will hit you. I keep cookies in my bedside table drawer because I wake up hungry several times a night."

He frowned. "This is not going to be the easy life I was imagining, is it?"

She shrugged. "I don't know. It might be different for you. Trippin' is really painful for me. For a few seconds right after, it feels like I've been hit by a Mack truck. Then the cold hits. That's the worst." She sighed heavily and turned back to the chore of putting her clothes up.

She touched a tag on one of her new shirts and got a flash from the saleslady who stocked the display. "Even the visions can be painful, depending on how long the contact with my subject is. Not to mention the pain that comes from what you see. That day at the station when you touched me, I saw your partner, Charlie, die. I was there with you, felt your pain. It was wrenching, heart rending." She turned as she said it and saw Balcher's eyes darken with the memory.

"That's what you're in for now, Balcher. Hunger that's never quenched for long, no matter how much you eat. Pain, anger, embarrassment or worse at the touch of another human being because—and you can bet your life on this—you'll see things in their hearts and souls that will tear you up inside. But mostly, there's the fear. Fear that if anybody ever realizes what you can do, that your life will be over. You can't share yourself with the world and it's the most alone feeling you can ever imagine. That's what being me is like."

"Not anymore, Spooky. You have me now," he said.

She laughed sarcastically. "That's really nice for me, Balcher. I'm definitely not the loser in all of this. Except that I can't help wondering how you'll feel six months down the road when it finally sinks in how much you've lost."

"Spooky, if you'll give my life a closer look, you'll see that I was not all that close to anyone before. Like you, I don't have much family. My best friend is Zack and I don't think that'll change because of this, but if it does? So what? Friendships change and grow anyway, regardless of what we do," he said, trying to reassure her.

"But did you have a death threat or worse hanging over your head? Ice Man won't give up until we're caught or he's dead." She said that last bit to get his reaction. She also needed the reminder because their current situation should be the only thing on their minds at the moment, not what could happen six months down the road.

"Not a problem," he stated calmly. "I hadn't intended on leaving the cold son of a bitch alive, anyway."

"You're not a murderer, Balcher," she said, his lack of emotion not what she had expected.

"No, I'm not. But he is. He shot me, remember? He's going to come after me again, and this time, I won't lose."

The doorbell rang startling Spooky, then she remembered the pizzas. "Food's here," she said, and then she flew by him to go pay the delivery man. For Spooky, the anticipation of food had been her only joy in life and just the thought of it always improved her mood exponentially.

"I'll do it," Balcher said, running to catch hold of her. "Can't be too careful." He went to the window by the door and peeked out. He recognized the delivery man as one who had delivered there last week when he had been watching Spooky. He opened the door, paid the guy and grabbed the pizzas.

Spooky took one of the boxes out of his hand and sat down on the couch. She didn't even go to the kitchen for a plate because just the smell of the food had her mouth watering. She fully intended to eat every last bite of this large pizza. She hadn't had anything since the Chinese place at the mall this afternoon and she was starving.

Balcher watched her eat and he was amused. Maybe not as amused as he would have been yesterday at this sight, but amused nevertheless. "So, not to ruin your appetite or anything, but what do you have in mind for the Ice Man. We can't wait too long, or he'll have the upper hand."

"We have to find him first," she said between bites. "Only way I know to do that, is to touch something he's recently touched." She took another huge bite, finishing off the first piece of her pizza. She licked her fingers.

"And how do we find something he touched?" Balcher asked, the image of her licking her fingers giving him ideas that had nothing whatsoever to do with the subject at hand.

"The safe at Radicom," she said, pulling another piece of pizza out of the box. "He was there trying to steal industrial secrets the other night when he nearly caught me."

She bit into the hot slice that was practically dripping cheese and then self-consciously wiped tomato sauce off the corners of her mouth with a paper napkin. "Radicom's security people knew somebody was out to steal the designs for their new assembly process. One of their own, they thought." She took another bite and chewed thoughtfully for a moment. "That's why I was there that night. We placed some old documents in an envelope and labeled it with the new process's name and hoped he'd take the bait. He did, although it wasn't one of Radicom's employees like we originally thought."

"So, the safe should have his fingerprints on it?"

She shook her head. "No, he wore gloves. But it may have a psychic imprint on it. Gloves don't help there."

"You just touch something he touched and you get his location?"

She smiled wryly. "Not always. But I might get flashes of things that mean something to him."

"Like you did with me that day when you saw Charlie die?"

She nodded. "Something at that moment must have brought his memory to you, and then you touched me and I saw it."

He frowned in concentration. "Yeah. I remember seeing everybody head for you when that woman started screaming. You looked so vulnerable and something about the whole thing made me think that you were under fire. I ran over to help you and you started to fall. Maybe I flashed on Charlie...well, I guess I did or you wouldn't have seen it, but I don't remember thinking about him."

"Our minds are funny things. A smell, a color, or maybe a few words is all it takes to bring things up out of our unconsciousness. We might not even know that we've dredged them up, but we're left with the emotions they evoke. A person can be totally happy at one moment and that happiness reminds us of another time in our life when we were that happy and then something about that time, say, the loss of someone dear to us, will make us sad all of a sudden. All these things pass through our minds in a split second and somehow we make sense of it all.

"However, when you're a clairvoyant, you get all of these images at the touch of a hand or some inanimate object and you have to figure out how to fit them together to find out what you're looking for."

Balcher made a face. "So what you're telling me is that even if you do read something of this guy's psychic imprint on the safe, it might not tell us anything we need to know to find him."

"The most important thing about the safe is that he had to be concentrating on his task, and maybe who he was working for. We might be able to backtrack from there."

"When do we go to Radicom?"

"Tonight," she said with her mouth full. She swallowed. "The sooner, the better. I'll call my Radicom contact and tell him that we'll be there."

"I'm going to need a weapon when we go looking for him, Spooky. At some point, I'll need to get into my apartment," he said.

"We'll figure that out later, but you do realize that you may have a better weapon at your fingertips, so to speak, right now?"

"Teleportation?"

"Maybe, or something even better."

"What could be better than that?" he asked.

"I don't know. Only you can find that out." She shrugged, still concentration on devouring her pizza.

Balcher went to the sofa to sit beside her. "How do you do it?" That question had been on his mind all day. If he could teleport, then how was he supposed to access the trigger to make it happen?

"You already know the answer to that," she said mysteriously.

"You forgot to say 'Grasshopper,'" he said with a half-smirk.

She frowned. "What?"

"You know, that old TV show with that actor, David Carradine, I think. Anyway, he plays this kid that's been taught karate and Eastern philosophy by this old Chinese dude, and then he ends up in America back in the old Western days. In the show, the kid would be kung-fu fighting all these bad guys and then right in the middle of all the action, he'd remember something that old Chinese dude said to him before he left, something inexplicable that the kid would have to figure out for himself, and that old guy always called him 'Grasshopper'," Balcher said, trying his best to mimic the accent.

"I never saw it," she mumbled, frowning.

"I only saw it in reruns on cable. Anyway, my point is that I don't have time to figure this out for myself. We have a time crunch here, in case you forgot," he said with raised eyebrows.

She rolled her eyes. "I didn't mean it that way. Look, this morning, a little while after you left me alone in my bedroom to think, you put a wall up to keep me from hearing your thoughts, and vice versa. How'd you do that?"

"I imagined a wall in my mind and there it was. Silence."

"That's how you do it. You imagine yourself where you want to be. I, personally, have a few words I think in my head. It kind of starts the process, if you know what I mean."

He looked at her curiously. "What are they?"

"Outta here."

"That's it?" he asked, amazed.

She shook her head. "That's it. Except I kind of scream it aloud in my head, and then I imagine myself back here."

"So, you're saying that if I imagine myself doing something, say teleporting, then it'll happen?"

"I'm saying, *if* you can do it, that's how it works." She looked around for something to drink and remembered she hadn't fixed herself anything.

"I'll get it," Balcher said, his mind still swimming with the information she just gave him. He got up and went into the kitchen. He grabbed a glass and was at the refrigerator pouring the iced tea when he realized that she hadn't asked for this aloud. She just thought of wanting it and he heard that. Or did she make him get up and get it for her?

He heard a giggle from the living room and cursed under his breath. "I heard that," he yelled, nearly spilling her drink. He took the glass to her and gave her an irritated look. "Did you make me do that?"

"Not intentionally." She giggled again. "I was thinking I wanted a glass of iced tea and you just jumped up and got me one. I think this mind reading thing might not be so bad, after all."

"So, you don't have this Jedi mind control thing going?"

"Not that I'm aware of," she said with a smile, but then the smile faded. "But, then again, I didn't know I was capable of changing people just by touching them, either," she murmured.

"You don't know that, yet," he reminded her.

"I do, too." Her eyes narrowed. "I thought you said you were with me today?"

"I was. Why? What happened?"

"Jenna Smith, a lady I helped a little while back. She had a missing husband, a cheating, lying, no good, scoundrel of a husband that I found in Reno with some rich bimbo. Anyway, she did my hair today. And yes, she was definitely changed. She is 'knowing things in her heart' and 'reading her customers desires for hair styles' now. It started right after I touched her."

"She had to touch you to do your hair. Did she 'see' anything when she touched you?"

Spooky shook her head. "I don't think so. I actually asked her if she got visions when she touched something. She said not. But that doesn't matter, she was changed."

"Did she appear unhappy with the way she is now?"

She frowned. "No. She seemed really happy. She has a new boyfriend and she told me she feels more confident about herself now. Like she's making better decisions, acting smarter."

"It looks like you gave her just enough to be able to read people better. That would give her an edge in dealing with the public and potential boyfriends," he said.

"I know. I don't really feel bad about what I did to her. It just made me nervous, you know, that I could have done something to her without even knowing it."

"How long was your contact with her? Back then, I mean," he

asked.

She scrunched her brow in thought. "I held her for a while. It was not something I usually do, but she grabbed me and held on and I felt sorry for her."

Balcher frowned. "In minutes, seconds. How long was it?"

"Thirty, forty seconds, I guess. Why?"

"That's a long time for you. You held onto that woman at the police station for ten seconds at the most. You were in contact with me even less." He frowned as he thought it out. "I got the ability to 'see' things without touching somebody from less than ten seconds. Your Jenna Smith held you for thirty seconds and she only got a general form of empathy from that."

"Empathy? How do you know that term?" she asked.

Balcher pointed to her book shelf on the far wall. There were countless books on the paranormal there. "I read up on the subject while you were gone today. I didn't have much else to do. You told me to think about all of this while you were gone, but I didn't have much except your preconceptions to go on."

"Find anything interesting?"

"I did see that people who study this stuff—at least as much as it can be studied with the scientific tools available today—think it's possible that psychic ability is inherited. I have a grandmother who had the sight, or so she claimed. Maybe, I was already 'wired' for psychic ability, but it was never activated until you touched me."

Spooky shut the pizza box and tossed it onto the coffee table. "Jenna said her uncle was psychic."

"Well, there you go," Balcher said. "She was wired for psychic ability, too. Maybe, not as complicated as you or I, but it was there nevertheless. You came into contact with that area of her brain when the two of you touched, and you saw something familiar and you reached out and...uh...activated it."

"So, you're saying that I only make what's there already start working, but that I don't do the actual wiring?" she asked dubiously.

"When you're only touching someone, yes. As for what happened when we tripped, that's got to be different. I mean, it's obvious that you changed me physically. Yourself, as well. But whether you made me capable of teleporting, I don't think we can count on that."

"But if I can teleport, then doesn't that mean that there are other human beings out there with that same 'wiring' already in their heads?"

"It's possible, yes. Think about it. The range of psychic abilities is amazing. There's telepathy, people who can read minds, and telekinesis, people who can move things with their minds. There are clairvoyants, like you, that can touch something or someone and see visions. There are people who can see the future, others that see dead people."

Spooky wiggled her eyebrows at him.

"I know, but don't knock it. I bet mediums would feel the same way about people who could teleport. That is, if they knew about them."

Spooky sighed. "I wondered when you'd get to that. In all my research, I only saw one mention of teleportation and it was mentioned only as a theory. There's no documented case of anyone ever having that ability. Remote viewing and astral projection, yes. Teleportation, no.

"Dean Koontz, an author who writes horror stories, wrote a book about a psychotic family where two of the brothers could teleport. That story didn't end well. At the end of the book, the sanest of the brothers grabbed the murderous one and teleported about a hundred times, one trip right after the other in quick succession, until they were physically merged together into a ball of writhing flesh and died," she said, despondent.

"And *Star Trek* postulates that in the twenty-fifth century people will have machines that will teleport human beings with the touch of a button," Balcher said wryly.

"You watch a lot of television, don't you?" she asked.

"And you don't?" he snorted, knowing that the Sci-Fi channel was almost her best friend.

"Okay! You got me there. But it still doesn't help us out here in the twenty-first century. So, let's say that we do take care of the Ice Man and live to tell about it. Next, we'll have to locate everybody I've ever worked for and find out what happened to them. I won't be able to rest until I do."

He nodded. "Then that's what we'll do. But, until then, try not to obsess on it too much. Those books of yours say that there are other factors that explain sudden psychic abilities in people."

"Yeah," she snorted. "A psychological shock, like rape, or a physical shock, such as a blow to the head. I'm in great company, aren't I?"

"If I had to choose from the three, I'd choose you, every time," he stated.

She slouched down into the cushions of the sofa, not entirely comforted by his words.

"Keep this in mind, sweetheart. If you only affect people that are already prone to be psychic, then the odds are that a large percentage of your clients were never wired psychically to begin with and have not been affected at all."

"What if everybody is prone, or 'wired' to be psychic, but only a few of us are born with the weird gene that activates it? What if I'm the equivalent of a psychic typhoid Mary infecting people with that weird gene like a virus?"

"Then we'll handle it, okay?" he assured her, feeling inept. He didn't know how else to help her. He didn't know enough about all of this, yet. "I do know one thing, Spooky. You have a good heart. So if you are infecting people with anything, it could be with your goodness. Didn't you say that Jenna was a much happier person since you changed her? I know you're worried about me, but I am better off because of you, too. I'd be dead if you hadn't risked your life for me. You knew it could kill you to trip again so soon, but you did it anyway."

"I was falling thirty floors to my death. I didn't have much of a choice but to teleport."

"But you did have the choice to bring me with you. For all you knew, you could have saved yourself, but bringing me with you would have been too much."

"Balcher, you'd just taken a bullet for me. If I'd let you fall and then I saved myself, I couldn't have lived with myself."

"I know that, sweetheart. That's what I'm trying to tell you. You're a good person. That's all any of us can hope for. If you have changed people without knowing it, we'll find those people, and then we'll do what we can to help them understand what they've become and how to live with it."

"You'll help me?" she asked with vulnerability.

"I'll help you," he agreed and pulled her into his arms. He hadn't held her since this morning and he needed the contact as much as she did. Their connection was not only mental; it seemed to be just as strong on the cellular level. A magnetic force to be reckoned with.

"This part of it amazes me," she murmured.

"What? Oh, you mean that you can touch me without visions flashing through your mind."

"Yeah. I've never been able to touch anyone, to hold anyone, without it exhausting me. With you, I feel strength coming into me in waves. It's just the most amazing thing." She snuggled deeper into his embrace.

"I feel the strength coming from you, too. Before, when I held someone like this it was a nice feeling, comforting. I didn't realize that this was underneath that feeling, only I didn't have the ability to see it." He propped his chin on Spooky's head, nestling her head against his neck. "Or maybe this wasn't there, never had been or would be, until I met you."

"Maybe, we were meant to be here, to be together," she murmured.

"You mean like fate? Or something else, a higher power?"

"There's something out there, I know that. I've gone through the lights too many times to doubt that."

"You mean God?"

She nodded her head. "Yes. An infinite power that directs my path when I'm in the lights and, I'm pretty sure, even when I'm not. When you're capable of seeing patterns in the world that others are not privy to, you understand that there is a bigger picture out there. All along my life there's been a definite path cut out before me. I've gone off the path a couple of times, just to see what happens, but all I seem to do is wonder around aimlessly until I find the path again."

She pulled her head away from him to look him in the face. "I should have realized that you were meant to play a significant part in my life. You've been the biggest obstacle on my path for a long time now."

"Obstacle?" he grunted, amusedly.

"Well, that's what I thought. Every time I've turned around for the last few years, there you were. If I'd been smarter, I would have known that you were there for a reason. To help me, not to hurt me."

"If you are so secure with the idea that a higher power is leading you through life, uh, your path as you call it, then why are you worried about the people you've touched in your past?"

"Because there's also the other power."

"The other power?" he said with a frown.

"The one with the shadows. I've named it Chaos, although others call it evil, or the devil, or Satan."

"Why Chaos?" he asked.

"Because it confuses, destroys, delights in ruining the beautiful patterns that the good higher power, God, places before me and around me."

"So, you're saying that evil is real?"

"Yes, it's real. The Ice Man had shadows all around him, didn't you notice?"

"I noticed the cold, but that's about it," he said, and then he frowned. "You were really cold after the trip. I felt it coming off of you in waves. Does that have anything to do with all of this?"

"Yes. It does in a way. You see, when I'm in the lights, I'm with the higher power, or God if you want a name. The process of coming out of that and hitting the mortal realm, so to speak, is so abrupt that I become cold down to my soul until my body becomes accustomed to being back."

"I thought that you didn't consider any of this magic, that you figured that there was a scientific explanation for what you go through?"

"It is scientific. Biology, even down to the cellular level is all about God. That's the thing that's so amazing. The pattern. Don't you see it?" she asked.

"I might, I guess, once we leave here." He looked over at the bookcase where he'd found those books on the paranormal earlier. "I saw that you had a Bible with your other books. Are you into organized religion?"

"The Bible is not a storybook. It's a historical account of a people who have found their lives impacted by something they don't understand. They call him God." She shrugged. "It's a story of good against evil and inside it is a road map for those who choose to follow it. Belief is the price of admission."

"Is that a good thing or a bad thing?" he asked.

"It's the only way it could work. If you don't believe God exists then you don't look for Him. If you're not looking, you can't find the pattern or path that He has placed before you. You let the shadows turn you this way and that, and before you know it, you're life is over and you didn't have the impact on this world that God intended."

"So, you're saying that we all still have a choice. That we don't have to follow any path set up for us?" he asked.

"Exactly. There's always a choice."

"But you've chosen to take the path chosen for you?"

"It's hard to explain," she sighed. "Think of a ceramic cup. Now, this cup wants to be a frying pan. So it sits on a hot flame one day until its molecules are heated up to the point that the ceramic glass shatters. What the cup wants doesn't really matter, does it? Because it's a cup, that's its purpose. Now the complexity of human nature makes us a little more complicated than the cup, but let's say that you see a child with an enormous capacity to play music. But for some reason, the kid gets it into his mind that he wants to play baseball and he sets his whole future on that path. He does well, maybe even plays a few years in the major league. But at some point in his life, he'll feel empty, because music is in his soul and he lost it. Unlike the cup that shatters in the flame, he may get a second chance to be happy. But he won't ever be what he could have been if he'd followed his intended path from the beginning."

She looked him solemnly in the eyes. "When we tripped together, you got to know me intimately, so you had a taste of what I'm talking about. Think about it. Since you know me so intimately, you probably think that you have a good idea what I should be like and how I should act. God, however, has known me intimately my whole life. He knows what my soul yearns for, what I will need to do to complete my life the way it was intended. I trust this power."

"And you're positive that this is not just a delusion from the trips?" he asked.

"I am. There's an intelligent consciousness out there that is inherently good. There's also one that is inherently evil. That condition places all of us in a constant struggle. When we choose good, we are helped along in our journey by this incredible power. When we choose evil, it destroys us. That's why I prefer the term Chaos, because that power can't help but turn in on itself. That is the nature of the beast, I guess you can say."

"Why didn't I see these beliefs inside you when we tripped? I saw everything else."

"Because you shared everything but my soul. You saw my mind, my memories, because they are imprinted on my brain in some form or fashion. But my soul is my own. So is yours. No matter what happens to us in the future, I can't choose your path for you, and you can't choose mine."

"But we can choose to be together," he stated.

"If our paths coincide, yes."

"And what if they don't." He frowned.

"Then that means there is something more important that we have to do than to stay together. But don't worry about that right now. If our paths separate in the future, it will be something that we see ahead of time and will understand."

"But how will we know that?"

"I don't know. I've never considered the possibility that I would share my life with anyone before. I think that I'll know...we'll *both* know it when we see it. God is not harsh; he will make it clear to us."

"Something is bothering me about all of this. If you're so sure that God will lead you into the correct path, and that you've been following this path for some while, then why are you so worried about touching those people in your past and changing them? Wouldn't that be part of God's plan?"

She shook her head, no. "Not necessarily, because the shadows are always around. They take you by surprise, especially if you get complacent and in a rut. I was so happy to have found a way to use my gifts to help people that for a while there, I just threw them around with little or no concern for their power. I told you that I've gone off the path several times. My casino run where I was gathering up money hand over fist was one of those times."

"So, helping casino owners was a bad thing?" he asked with a smirk.

"Do you gamble?" she asked, her head cocked to one side.

"No. I have better things to do with my money than to give it to the casinos."

"Exactly. So, when I help a casino owner keep a card-counter out of his establishment, I'm essentially helping an entity who takes money legally from desperate people in order to catch someone that is illegally stealing from the entity. Not something to be really proud of. When I walk into a casino, I see Chaos all around. Lights flashing, bells ringing, people shouting in triumph one moment and disgust the next. Shadows move consistently through the hoards of people, touching this one and avoiding the next one. I don't like those places, but I do a good bit of my work in them."

"And that's off of your path?"

"It's not always that clear. I think that some dark patches are mandatory for everyone, or else how would we know when we're going in the right direction." She sighed. "You'll have to discover all of this on your own. It will make more sense to you when you've faced choices of your own."

"So when do we start?" he asked.

"Tonight. Once we leave the sanctity of my house, things will be put into motion. There won't be any turning back. I just ask one thing of you. Trust your instincts. Your life and mine may depend on how you use these new powers of yours."

"I found that out yesterday at the casino." He pulled away from her and stood up. "No time like the present. Let's go take a look at that safe." He held his hand out to Spooky and she placed her hand in his.

She took in a deep breath and let it out. She felt safe here, safer than she's ever known. But stepping out of that front door was definitely part of her path, and she could tell by the way the door was pulsating—it was not the subtle quiver she saw only an hour ago—that it was time.

If she were to try and describe this phenomenon to Balcher, he would think she was crazier than he is already starting to think. He needed to see it for himself.

He might fight the idea that something out there knew what was good for him and was willing to lead him towards it—God knows she certainly had times where she chose not to take the path chosen for her out of stubbornness or curiosity—but in time, he would see that he still had choices. That this higher being left a lot of what he chose to do on a daily basis up to him and only put signs, like the pulsating door, there when his choice was potentially soul changing.

"Okay, let's go," she said, standing up and squaring her shoulders. "Let's go find that monster and put him out of his misery."

Chapter Eleven

They walked into the Radicom office at nine o'clock. It was not totally dark outside yet, but Spooky felt the shadows slithering around and it felt dark to her. They met the security guard at the front desk and he led them upstairs as he was previously advised to do.

Spooky walked into the outer office of the president where she'd been before, and immediately felt the change in atmosphere. She ignored it for the time being and went through the door to the office of the head honcho himself. The safe was behind his desk on the wall behind a picture. Not imaginative, but practical.

"Do you have the combination to the safe?" Balcher asked in a whisper, staying close beside her.

"No, but I don't need it," she answered, pulling the picture away from the wall. It was attached by hinges on the left side of the safe and opened up like a door.

"Just touching the safe will be enough to get what you need?"

"Maybe, maybe not. But I'm going to open the safe anyway, just to be sure."

"But how—" Balcher started, then he shut up when he saw her touch the safe and go into that trance he remembered all too well.

The glazed look was gone within seconds and she breathed deeply. "I know who he works for," she said as her fingers manipulated the old-fashioned dial of the safe to five different numbers and then pulled the thick metal door open. She put her hands on top of the documents inside of the safe and went into that trance again. This time it didn't even take a few seconds. She shook her head as if to clear it and then she closed the safe door and locked it. She put the picture back into place, as well.

"How'd you do that? What'd you see?" he asked, curiosity nearly killing him.

"Not enough," she said answering his second question first. She'd let him think about the answer to the first question himself. It shouldn't be that difficult. Every time the owner of the safe opened it, he was thinking the combination. That was the most prominent imprint left on the safe. "The fake document we used to lure him here was not in the safe. Nothing else in there had any imprint from our guy."

"Why didn't you let me try?" he asked, feeling a tiny bit of aggravation. She hadn't even offered him the chance to try. How was he going to find out if he could do it, if she wouldn't give him a chance?

She felt the censure in his voice and in his thoughts. "Because the psychic imprint left by the Ice Man was like a static charge left on a carpet. I come along and that static charge is discharged by me. You can walk on that same carpet, but unless the charge has built back up again—or in our case, if the guy came back and left another imprint—you would feel nothing."

"Then why didn't you let me try it first?"

Her eyebrows went up. "Because you don't have the experience to understand and make sense of the jumbled images you might see, yet. If you'd discharged the psychic charge left by our target and didn't understand what you saw, then I couldn't go behind you and try again."

"How am I supposed to learn without practicing?" He was still annoyed.

"You can practice. On other things. Believe me, there will plenty of chances. If you have been given the gift of clairvoyance, you'll start getting flashes just by touching things: a door knob, a hand rail. After a while, you'll stop touching those things just because of the flashes.

It'll be an unconscious choice, but it'll be the only way you can protect yourself," she explained.

"Protect myself from what?" he asked, following her from the office to what looked like a secretary's office.

"From the confusion. The first time it happens, you'll see what I mean. It's like seeing a movie flash right before your eyes and it blinds you to what you're actually seeing at the time. Try walking or driving with your eyes closed, that's as close as I can explain it," she murmured, heading for the potted palm she hid behind that night.

She felt the cold immediately, even before any contact. If just standing in the same spot the Ice Man stood in could do this to her, then touching something he touched was going to be a jolt. She hesitantly reached out to touch the leaves of the palm and the moment her fingers came into contact with green waxy surface of the plant, her body jerked as if she'd gotten an electrical shock. In that split second, she was pulled into his head, seeing the scene from his eyes as if she was there in the moment.

He approached the plant with the knife gripped firmly in his hand. He was eager, excited at the intrusion, the opportunity to use his knife giving him an erection. He anticipated the blood, the power, the ecstatic release he would feel as he thrust his blade into living flesh, male or female, it didn't matter. He swung at the palm, knocking it out of his way, and saw no one. There was a pile of clothes, a backpack. A camera lay at his feet with strewn dirt and leaves. He reached down and picked it up. Then it hit him.

Shock. Dread. Cold, cold, fear.

Spooky's skin erupted in goose bumps as ice flowed through her veins.

She released the palm abruptly and stumbled back. Pulling out of his memory was like being jerked out of a frozen lake and thrown into a hot sauna bath. Her skin was tingling. She felt a distinct pop in her ears, like that of coming down fast from a high altitude, as she wrenched herself back to the present. Sliding her hands up and down her arms in an effort to make the chills dissipate, she staggered to the other side of the room and fell shaking onto the couch put there for visitors.

"What'd you see?" Balcher asked, even though he had gotten some of that second hand. He was staring at the palm, eyes hypnotically drawn to the plant and he couldn't stop himself from reaching out and touching it just like Spooky did moments ago.

Spooky watched with horror, but was too dazed to stop him. She didn't want his first vision to be one so devastatingly powerful. If he was clairvoyant, he would get slammed by this one because she pulled away before the powerful imprint was fully discharged. She couldn't help it, she couldn't bear touching that coldness any longer.

"Son of a bitch—" Balcher yelped and then jumped away from the plant. He was shaken. He turned on her suspiciously. "I thought you said I couldn't get a vision from an object after you touched it?"

Her voice was weak. "Normally, no. But this one was powerful and I pulled out of it before it was finished with me."

He moved across the room and sat down beside her. His eyes were glazed with what he'd just seen. "He's afraid of you."

"I know. He intends to catch me, and if that isn't possible, he's going to kill me. He figures that my dead body would be worth almost as much as if he were to take me in alive."

"You got all of that just now? I just saw his intent to kill you and then his fear when he realized what you'd done," Balcher said, amazed.

She frowned. "Yeah, I got that, too. But then, I guess, I pushed beyond that and connected with him somehow. This imprint was so strong that it formed a trail to his mind and I followed it. Hopefully, I can eventually follow it to where he is."

"That's what you meant by having experience in using the visions, isn't it?" he asked. "The ability to see beyond the actual vision?"

Spooky pushed herself off the couch. She wanted out of this office. She headed for the door and then for the elevator. She didn't speak again until they were headed down to the lobby. "Yeah, that's what I meant. In time, you'll gain experience and you'll see what I mean. For now, though, I need you to trust me."

The elevator door opened and they walked into the lobby. They signed out at the security guard's desk, and then left the building. The night air was calm, balmy, but Spooky still had goose bumps.

"Come here," Balcher said, opening his arms.

There, even though they looked conspicuous in the parking lot, Spooky moved into his arms and held on tightly. Again she felt the waves of warm comfort spread through her system, like snuggling into a warm blanket. Her shivering decreased and the goose bumps went away.

"I'm not sure I could ever give this up," she murmured, pulling out of his arms reluctantly and heading for the car they had rented earlier that night. Her car was still at the casino and she felt danger associated with the thought of going back to it for the time being.

Balcher got into the driver's seat and turned to her before cranking the car. "Why don't I feel anything when I touch this steering wheel?" His mind was still spinning with what he'd done in the office. It had his juices going.

"Are you sure you don't?" she asked.

"What do you mean?"

"Concentrate. Hold the wheel with both hands and kind of let your mind go."

Balcher closed his eyes and tried clearing his mind. Then something did come to him. In his mind he saw himself turning and smiling at a woman sitting beside him in the front of the car. It was just a quick flash, but it was real. The man was excited, this was their first trip to Las Vegas.

Balcher let go of the wheel and opened his eyes. "I saw a couple visiting from Texas, I think. A man and his wife, and it was their first time in Vegas." Then he frowned. "Why did I have to concentrate to see that? Why didn't it just pop into my head?"

"Be grateful for small favors," Spooky said with a smile. "If you saw something every time you touched an object, your life would be hell."

Nodding, he cranked the car and then pulled out of the parking lot. He glanced at her briefly. "I saw what he was feeling right then, while he was driving. Is that how it usually is?"

She nodded. "Most of the time, yeah. You have to push through—follow the connection—to get more than general impressions."

"What do you mean, 'follow the connection'?"

Spooky should have known that he wouldn't leave the subject alone. "Your first impressions are kind of like a dog that gets a scent. You know the person has been there; you may even see what they were thinking or doing at the time. But then, like the dog, you have to follow the scent or 'connection' to find out more."

"And that's how you find missing persons?"

"That's actually a little more complicated."

He glanced her way for a second. "What do you mean?"

"Connections are everywhere. Husbands and wives are connected. Fathers and daughters, mothers and sons, sisters and brothers, well, you get the drift. To a lesser extent, objects are connected with people, especially if they have significant sentimental value to that person. Anyway, when a person goes missing, I don't have that person there to read, obviously, so I have to make do with an object or one of their loved ones," she explained.

"How does it work? I mean, how do you follow a connection?"

"Connections are invisible, like love, like faith, but they're real. Think about it. You have people in your life that you are connected to. But, say, one day you decided to just pick up and leave without a word to anybody, never to return. What do you think would happen?"

"I can't imagine myself doing that. I have responsibilities, people I care about. I couldn't hurt them that way."

"Exactly. Connections. Whether you like it or not, you are tethered by strong invisible strands to your life and the relationships you've built. You couldn't leave without damaging those connections. The problem is, they don't break. They're always there. You'll always feel them no matter where you go, and the people you left behind will feel them, too. That's the connection I follow to find missing people. Psychic energy can see those connective threads and follow them as surely as sound travels through telephone wires."

"But, what if they're dead?"

"The connection still exists. I've found many graves over the years. Just because a person dies, it doesn't mean they're forgotten. Have you ever worked a missing persons case?" she asked.

"A few. Especially when foul play is expected," he answered.

"People know when their loved ones have died. They may not acknowledge it, denial is a strong emotion, but deep down inside, they know it. The connection changes abruptly and they feel the loss, not of the connection, but of hope. They come to me needing closure and their sheer determination makes the connection stronger. That's why so many people choose to bury their loved ones instead of cremation." she said.

"Really? I would have imagined it's because of religious reasons.

They want their loved one's bodies in one piece when they go to meet God."

She shook her head to the negative. "They know their loved ones will end up as a handful of dust at some point, so no, that's not the main reason. Doesn't the Bible say, 'Ashes to ashes, dust to dust?'"

"I think so," he said.

"I believe the main reason is because of the connection they still feel towards their loved ones. Check out any cemetery and you'll find graves tended lovingly, flowers changed, toys, angels, letters, left on headstones. The connection definitely survives death. As long as there is someone alive that remembers a person, their connection to this world doesn't end."

"I thought that love was just an abstract idea, but you're saying that it is real, a physical energy that you can tap into and follow?"

"It's real. Just as good and evil are real. Just as God and his antithesis, whether you call him Satan or the devil or whatever is real. All of these things can be seen and felt and it doesn't take a psychic to do it. Psychics just have a little more insight into the area because we can sometimes see a physical manifestation of the energy," she said.

"This is totally confusing," he muttered.

"Not really. You and every other human being that ever lived has had access to all of this energy all along, only it was felt and not seen. The only difference is that you may be able to see it now."

Balcher let that bit of information sink into his brain.

"I bet you're hungry again, aren't you?" she asked, changing the subject. He's had more than enough to think about for now.

"Yeah. I can't believe it. I just ate a little over an hour ago."

His stomach growled and Spooky giggled. "Welcome to my world, Balcher. A vision devours calories. You just had two and one of them was a doozey. You'd better stop at a drive through somewhere and get us both something to eat. We've got a long way to go tonight before we're finished."

He pulled into a McDonald's and ordered himself a couple of Big Mac's and super-sized fries. Spooky copied that order and they sat in the parking lot munching away at their food.

"I can't believe this," Balcher said. "I'll never again have to feel guilty for eating."

"It's not all it's cut out to be," she murmured. "The constant hunger gets old fast."

He grunted and took his second burger out of its box. "So, besides the constant hunger, what are the other downsides to these visions?"

Spooky shrugged, "Imagine you're going down steps and you touch the rail and suddenly get a vision. You lose your balance and take a tumble because you couldn't see that next step."

"Wow. That's happened to you?"

"Yeah, a couple of times. I'm lucky I haven't broken my neck, I guess."

"So, how do you stop that?"

"Don't use the rail," she said, with a shrug.

"Sounds simple," he said with a grin. "What else?" he asked, curious.

"Well, it's difficult emotionally when you see something bad," she answered.

He nodded. "Like when you saw Charlie die that day you touched me?"

"Yeah, like that. Or when I saw a client's little girl being molested by her own father. Or when I saw a teen-aged girl cutting herself to relieve the pain in her soul. Or when I saw—"

"That's enough," he said, cutting her off. "I literally get the picture." He put his carton of fries down, the images she evoked bringing her actual memories of those instances to his mind and stifling his appetite.

"You'd better finish those," she told him, still munching on her own. "You'll need the fuel later."

"This is a roller-coaster ride, isn't it? Highs and lows all the time."

"Not all the time. You have to allow yourself a good bit of down time to recuperate. I think that's why I did so much casino work. It was depressing work, but not as exhausting as the other stuff. And it helped me have enough money to make sure I'd never be hungry. As you can imagine, I have a huge food bill," she admitted with a smile.

He smiled because it was not difficult to imagine, at all. "Everything I've learned from you today seemed familiar to me. Like I'd read it in a book somewhere a long time ago, but forgot it until you reminded me. It's getting increasingly more difficult to access your memories."

What about hearing me think?

She put the words out there, hoping the ability to read each other's minds was there to stay. They would need that edge during the next few days.

"Yes, I can still hear your thoughts," he answered her aloud. "And yes, that'll definitely come in handy. So, where to next?" he asked, starting the car.

They pulled around the parking lot and waited in line behind another car that was turning left into traffic. Spooky decided to take this moment to test him on something further. "Look both ways and tell me if either of the directions feels different or special to you."

Balcher gave her a hard look and then did as she requested. He looked both ways. To start with, nothing stood out. Then, not sure if he was noticing something or if he was just imagining it, he noticed that the road to the right was alarmingly clear, but the road to the left was kind of blurred. No, blurred wasn't the word. It just wasn't as intense as the other direction.

"I'm supposed to go right?" he asked, feeling like a student taking a test.

Spooky smiled. "Why? Tell me exactly what you see."

He shrugged and pulled up to the edge of the drive to wait for a hole in the traffic. "It looks a lot clearer," he said, and then he accelerated, turning right out of the parking lot.

As he drove, he began to see a clear path ahead of him. It was barely noticeable, something he would never have thought about if she hadn't pointed it out to him. It was like the light was a smidge brighter, the colors a dab sharper. His heart began to beat faster as he followed the path. He could barely take his eyes away from it long enough to give Spooky a flabbergasted look.

"This is the path you mentioned? I thought you were talking about something abstract. This is physical...something I can see! Is this what you see all the time?"

"Not all the time, no," she shook her head. "Not even ninety percent of the time, if I had to put a number on it. During most of your life there will be choices that won't affect the outcome of your life one way or the other. Like, if you were deciding between Mexican or Chinese food, or buying one brand of soap verses another. You won't get any help deciding between car insurances or toilet papers, even if one of them turns out to be the wrong decision and gives you a serious rash on your butt. The only time this happens is when your life is about to change drastically. It's more of a 'heads up' than a road map."

"But this gives us an advantage, doesn't it?" he asked.

"Not necessarily," she said. "I have a feeling that the other side—the Chaotic side—has the same advantage, except their side sees shadows to lead them. This is not something that happens to me because I'm special. It happens to everyone, even non-psychics. Think about it. Even before I touched you that day, I bet you had hunches, or feelings, that convinced you to take one direction over another. You followed one lead or clue on a case that shouldn't have necessarily have meant anything, except that you saw it and it wouldn't let go of you. Am I right?" she asked, looking at him from the passenger seat.

He glanced at her briefly. "Yeah. I've had hunches. Some of them didn't seem promising, but they stayed on my mind until I checked them out. Most—but not all—of the time, they'd lead me to something more concrete that I could take to a District Attorney," he agreed with a hint of astonishment.

"And," she added, "I bet you've had times where you felt the hairs on the back of your neck stand up, or had the prickly feeling that you were being watched and it put you on alert?"

"That's happened to me a bunch of times, especially when you were around, but other times, too. Are you saying that this is normal for everybody?"

"As far as I have been able to tell, yes. In times of crisis, most people have something that tells them what to do. They may not trust the instinct—or higher power, if you choose to call it that, or even their inner consciousness—but it's there. And, if you were to ask them afterwards what made them choose the one path that saved their lives, they'd tell you that in the midst of the accident, fire, robbery, etcetera, that their choice all of a sudden became crystal clear to them."

"So I've been seeing this path my whole life, but never recognized it?" he said with disappointment.

"Probably. Maybe not as clear as it is now, but it was there," she said as the glitz of the city could now only be seen in their rear view mirrors.

They took a road that headed towards a small airport outside the city limits and they were only a mile away from it when Balcher asked, "The airport? Oh, we're going to Atlanta to find the people that hired the Ice Man to steal Radicom's information, aren't we?" he asked, actually seeing that information blazing in her head like a billboard, even though she'd never mentioned any of it aloud.

Spooky nodded.

He was introspective for a moment, then he frowned. "Wait! We can't fly anywhere. We don't have any I.D."

"We don't need it. I know a pilot that'll take me anywhere in the United States without question. He has a small plane in one of the back hangars at the airport."

"That's illegal," Balcher said, still thinking like a cop. In this day and age, it was not good to have pilots willing to fly people around without identification. The guy had to be dirty.

"He's not," Spooky answered his unspoken question. "He's a client of mine, a really good man. I touched one of his passengers in a casino once and saw the guy die. He was killed in Derek's plane when it went down. I tracked the plane down from the numbers on the tail panel in my vision and then I came out here and talked with the owner of that plane. Derek was skeptical, but he let me touch his plane. Luckily, I was able to see enough for him to figure out what might be wrong with it. He checked the part—I can't remember now exactly what it was, some internal part of the engine, I think—and nearly turned white when he saw it. I think he knew that I'd just saved his life."

"Still, it's not right," Balcher insisted.

"He's got copies of my driver's license and one of my credit cards," Spooky assured him. "With my circumstances, I thought it best if he kept those on hand. That way, I'd never have to worry about being caught without ID like I am now."

Balcher let that thought settle a bit. He didn't suppose they had much choice. Then something hit him about what she'd just said. "You said you saw that guy die. That's precognition—seeing the future! How many gifts do you have?"

Spooky heard the horrified excitement in his voice. "I've seen events in the future precisely three times. And before you ask, no, I don't go around seeing people die all the time. That was a fluke. I don't know if I'd count precognition as one of my gifts, specifically."

Balcher's eyebrows met in the middle and Spooky could feel his mind grinding from where she sat across from him. He was beginning to hit the point where learning anything more was likely to be too much. Unfortunately, he was going to have to press through that point if they were going to make it out of this alive.

"Those books of yours, you know, the ones on psychic abilities?" he asked throwing a glance at her before putting his eyes back on the road. "They say that it's rare to see a psychic with more than one ability. Yet, here you are with three of them, and one of them has never before been recorded in human history. Something's stranger than strange here, Spooky."

Spooky felt her heart lurch. She wondered when he'd catch on to that. "You're right. There is, although I was hoping to wait for a later time to explain that part of it to you. Can it wait until we get on the plane?" she asked, hoping for a moment to gather her thoughts. Then she remembered. He could hear her thoughts.

As a test, she imagined that wall that Balcher had used yesterday to close himself off from her. She placed it around her thoughts and then practically shouted in her mind, *My mother was a lab experiment!*

She looked at Balcher and realized that he hadn't heard a thing! Then he frowned. Oh, well, she guessed it was just too good a thing to work for her.

"I see your wall," he said, startling her. "If you don't want me to know what you're thinking, then that's fine by me."

He didn't hear her! And he was sulking! That made Spooky smile. "I was testing something you taught me yesterday," she said. And then, to salve his feelings she added, "I want you to know why I'm so different, or at least, what I was told about my conception, but I don't want to be interrupted in the middle of it. Let's get on the plane first, and then I will explain it all to you."

He didn't like it, she could tell that from the expression on his face even though she could not read his mind. Her wall apparently worked both ways.

That was okay, because she needed this silence. Having the ability to read someone's mind was like having a constant conversation. It was tiring.

They rode the rest of the way in silence and Balcher was still quiet when they entered the hangar to look for Derek. The woman behind the desk recognized Spooky and was happy to call Derek and tell him she needed an emergency flight.

An hour later, when they were in the air and settled into their seats, Spooky finally summoned the courage to speak up.

"My mother was brilliant. She had an I.Q. of one hundred and eighty and an aptitude for knowing things, small things about people. The word in paranormal circles for this kind of ability is 'adept.' It's sort of an ability to pluck bits of information out of the air. Anyway, my mother was a lonely soul, her intelligence setting her apart from most people, and that loneliness got worse when her parents—my grandparents—were killed in a car crash when she was seventeen. She was left with no close family, although I think I have some second or third cousins in Idaho. She wasn't close to them and so I never was, either.

"Anyway, since my grandparents were wealthy, she was left pretty well off financially. And with her brains and money, she had the choice of any school in the country. She decided on a university in California because of her obsession with the paranormal, *and* because of a certain professor who taught at that school and who was, at that time, at the forefront of paranormal research. You might recognize his name from one of the books in my library so I'm not going to mention his name, if you don't mind.

"Needless to say, this professor glommed onto my mother from almost the moment she stepped foot onto that campus. It was 1978 when she met up with him, and by 1980, they were lovers. Her money, her beauty and her fledgling psychic abilities were more than he could resist, I guess. So, they moved in together.

"I don't know all that happened between them, because my mother wouldn't tell me everything, but she did tell me a few things—not that I understood any of it then—after I teleported that first time."

Spooky laughed in derision as she thought back on that time when she was five years old. "Can you imagine hearing your boyfriend—not the professor at this point, he was long gone—tell you that your little girl disappeared into thin air right in front of him? Oh, he didn't tell her what he was trying to do to me, and he probably wouldn't have said anything at all if he hadn't been stoned to the gills and ranting at her as he packed up his bags and ran out on her," Spooky said disgustedly before shaking the memory off.

"Anyway, getting back to the professor and hopefully to try and make a long story short, she told me about an experiment this guy talked her into performing in order to enhance her psychic abilities. He put her on a drug cocktail of LSD, cocaine, marijuana, speed, and Quaaludes. God, you name it and he tried it, not to mention all of the supposed legal drugs like valium and other stuff used for depression. Of course, neither of them even considered the fact that she could become pregnant with me during the time they began experimenting, but, if you ask, me, it wouldn't have stopped him from using her. It might have even made her more exciting to him.

"To my mother's credit, when she realized she was pregnant, she tried to call it all off. He was furious, screaming at her for not being willing to take their research to the highest level. But since most of her money was gone by then and he hadn't seen any improvement in her psychic abilities, I am assuming at this point that he didn't want to mess with her any longer. He tossed her out.

"So, there's my mother; pregnant, alone, broke and addicted to cocaine. She had me six months later and we survived one way or the other for the next six years until she was caught trying to burglarize an electronics' store." She looked at Balcher and met the sympathetic expression on his face. "She was so smart, she could have been anything she wanted. That guy destroyed her. Chaos," she said, matter-of-factly.

"You loved her," Balcher said, the knowledge deep in his heart. He had remembered her story along with her and the pain of it was difficult to deal with.

"I really did," she said. "It's hard to imagine, but she was a part of me, similar to the way you are now. I know the pain she suffered for her addiction. Unfortunately, prison didn't break her of the habit. She did things there with the guards and they provided her with the stuff. When she got out, it was less than two years before she was dead of an overdose. There was nothing I could do to change her path, although I tried." She shrugged. "She preferred the shadows. Pain often does."

"It's hard to believe that one human being can do something like that to another human being," he said, referring to the professor.

"You're forgetting Hitler and his army of doctor's performing their atrocities in the concentration camps. And ask yourself how many so-called scientists there are now who can't resist the temptation of messing around with DNA in order to create the perfect fighting machine, or maybe a human being that will never get sick or one that ages three or four times slower than the normal human being."

Spooky's hand gripped onto the armrest of her chair when the plane hit an air pocket. "And, if we're not successful in stopping the Ice Man, some deliriously happy scientist is gonna have us in his lab experimenting till his ol' heart is content."

"I feel like I've landed right smack in the middle of a horror novel," Balcher grumbled.

He meant that as a joke, but Spooky didn't find it at all funny. It was too close to being true.

He grasped her hand. "I'm sorry, I shouldn't have said that."

"Hey, laughing about it is better than crying about it, I guess," she said, forgiving him.

He squeezed her hand gratefully. "Getting back to the present, how do you know that we'll find something of value in Atlanta?" he asked.

"We were led in this direction. We wouldn't have been sent this way without reason. Either there's some information of significant value to be found in Atlanta, or we are being placed out of the reach of danger for the time being. It won't be a wasted journey."

"What if you have to touch someone to get the information we need?" he asked, referring to her fear of 'infecting' another human being with the psychic gene.

She nodded. "I've been thinking about that. Earlier this evening, I touched that palm frond and got the same information you got, except that I must have pushed further or I wouldn't have gotten the rest of it. If I can figure out a way to hold myself back, maybe I can get what we need without making a connection."

The plane hit another air pocket and Spooky squeezed Balcher's hand tight.

"You hate flying so much, I'm surprised you haven't considered teleporting," he said with amusement.

She smiled. "The embarrassment of showing up naked and moneyless makes that one a no-brainer."

"You brought me along on your last trip through the lights," he said, unknowingly referring to the phenomenon with the same name Spooky had used over the years. "Why are you so afraid to try bringing along clothes and a billfold?"

She looked at him like he was crazy. "You can look in a mirror and still ask me that?"

He laughed. "All right, you have a point. But it still occurs to me that you may have more control over all of this than you're aware of. I came out of that last trip without a hole in my chest. And the ol' ticker's been working fine ever since. The changes you just alluded to were actually beneficial to both of us. I didn't come out of the trip with boobs or without my..." he dropped the end of that sentence on purpose, looking down and wagging his eyebrows comically.

"Heaven forbid," she said, giggling. "But, for all you know, you could have one of my ovaries in there." She looked pointedly at his stomach.

He frowned. "Dammit! You just had to say that didn't you? I'm getting an x-ray as soon as all of this is over," he grumbled.

"I was just kidding!" She laughed. Balcher was acting the fool just to amuse her, to lighten her heart, and she knew it. It was certainly working. She hadn't laughed so much in a long time, if ever.

Balcher was the best thing that ever happened to her, there was no doubt about that. Then her smile faded and she instinctively put her wall back up, except that this time she imagined a three inch glass wall in the place of the stone one that Balcher had used this morning. It was obvious that he resented it when she shut herself off from him. Maybe he wouldn't notice this wall.

With that done, she allowed the depressing thoughts to come in. She was not the best thing that had ever happened to Balcher, and it would only be a matter of time before he realized that. As soon as all this mess was over, he was going to go back to his life and find that he no longer fit there, that his world had changed irrevocably and there was no way to change it back.

He's the kind of man that takes what's thrown at him and lives with it. He won't complain, or rail uselessly against fate, he will just accept it. And, he will accept her, because she was part of it. Not that he would have a choice, she was essentially the only game in town.

No. He didn't deserve what happened to him because of her. He didn't deserve it, at all.

Chapter Twelve

Except for one stop for fuel, the rest of their plane trip was uneventful. They landed at a small airport outside of Atlanta and hired a cab to take them to a hotel, but not before making the cabbie stop at an all-night fast food joint where they loaded up on several items from their fattening menu.

After checking into the hotel, they planned their mission for the next morning over a table covered with onion rings and chili-dogs. The man they sought would not find their interest at all favorable and was not likely to be cooperative. Of course, that wouldn't stop two psychics, especially two that were as determined as Spooky and Balcher were.

It was close to four o'clock in the morning, Georgia time, when they finished their planning and the last of the onion rings. Spooky cleaned up while Balcher showered and then she hit the shower herself.

With her tummy full and the warmth of the recent shower easing her tired body, Spooky didn't see any problems with falling asleep tonight. She pulled on her bra and panties and then left the bathroom. Balcher was already in bed, so she turned out all the lights and collapsed exhaustedly in the huge king sized bed knowing that eight o'clock was going to come early in the morning.

But sleep didn't come quickly for either of them.

"Spooky?" Balcher asked in the darkness.

"Hmm?"

He turned on his side to face her. "That wall thing, you know, the way you shut off from me tonight? Well, I just wanted you to know that I understand why you did it. Some things are private. I didn't mean to act all pissed off like I did."

She sighed and reached out her hand to touch him. The contact enhanced their connection, making their thoughts and feelings clearer. "I know that," she said, staring up at the ceiling in the semi-darkness. The hotel room, with the lights from the city coming through the slats of the blinds, was not as dark as she liked it at home. Then she turned on her side so that they were face to face. "You're a guy," she said with a sigh.

"God, I hope so," he said with a chuckle.

"A smart ass, but still a guy," she said bemusedly. "So, being a guy and all, I would have thought you would understand the need for silence every once in a while. Isn't that a typically male thing? Being strong? Silent? Macho? Anyway, while I like the open communication most of the time, there are times when I need privacy."

"Like when you need to pass gas, or something, and don't want me to know it?" he quipped with a laugh.

Spooky rolled her eyes. "You are definitely a guy," she muttered, rolling onto her back.

He laughed and then leaned over her. "Not that it would help, I'd smell it," he said tongue in cheek. "With all that we've eaten in the last twenty-four hours, I'm surprised that subject hasn't come up yet."

Spooky could hear the marvel in his voice. What was it with guys and their fascination with bodily functions? "Yes, well, so I guess you can see that there will be reasons for putting the wall up?"

"I guess so. I think it's the image of the wall that gets my back up. Why don't we try imagining a mute button? It has a more comical intonation."

"A mute button?"

"Yeah, a big red button with the word 'mute' on it. Why don't you try it?"

She did. And then she made herself think of a little ditty that their recent conversation brought to mind.

Beans, beans, good for the heart, the more you eat? The more you—

"Fart!" Balcher said, laughing hysterically.

"Well, I guess that didn't work," she growled.

He recovered himself, barely. "Okay, so it didn't. Then I guess the wall will have to be it. The thing I don't like is that one of us may have the wall up and the other one might have an emergency and need to speak up. What do we do in that case?"

"Knock?"

"What?"

"Imagine a door in the wall and knock on it," she said.

"Okay, you put up a wall and then think something. I'll see if I can read you. If I can't, then I'll imagine a door and knock on it."

She put her wall up, the visible one from Balcher's imagination, and then sent a thought out.

Men are control freaks!

"Well, did you get anything?" she asked aloud.

"No."

"Okay. Try knocking."

Nothing was happening. She wished she could see Balcher's face a little more clearly. He could be turning purple or something with the effort. Then she felt a thud in her mind. It was strange, but she supposed that it could have been a knock.

"Did you feel that?"

"I felt something, a thud, but it was faint," she answered. "Why don't you try it now? Put up your wall and let me see if I can knock on your door."

The wall went up.

Silence.

"Did you hear that?" he asked.

"Nope," she said shaking her head. "Okay, here goes."

She saw his wall in her mind and she imagined a door in the middle of it. She imagined a fist and slammed it against the door.

"Owwww!" he yelped, sitting up in the bed beside her. "Not so hard!"

"You felt that," she asked amazed.

"It sounded like a cannon going off in my head," he growled. "From now on, a soft knock will do." He massaged his temples and then shook his head the way people do when they're trying to clear water out of their ears.

She giggled. "Sorry. I guess I'm going to have to hold back on you, you big baby."

He growled and then rolled over on top of her, holding most of his weight up by placing his elbows onto the mattress on either side of her. "I'll teach you something about holding back," he promised as he leaned in for a kiss.

Spooky reached up to meet him. She'd been waiting for this all day. This compulsion to touch Balcher, to feel his skin under her fingertips and his long hard body against hers, was never ending. They could barely stand two feet from each other without feeling the magnetic force pulling them together. Sex with him was more than she had ever imagined it could be, especially with the traumatic incident she had as a child being her one and only experience with the subject.

Oh, she'd experienced the act second-hand many times. Those experiences were unintended, obviously—she would never have ventured into anyone's sexual memories by choice—but they gave her a general sense of what was good and what was bad about sex.

With Balcher, sex was a mind-shattering occurrence, emotionally and physically. Her lips tingled where they touched his. The stroke of his fingertips where they lightly flitted over her skin as they moved down her body was enough to make the nerves under her skin thrum like the strings of a guitar.

He pushed her bra straps down her shoulders to uncover her breasts and then he looked at her solemnly, as if studying an object of art. Her nipples contracted and then hardened in anticipation of the touch of his mouth. She unconsciously arched her back off of the bed to bring them closer to him.

Balcher leaned down and took one of the pert nipples into his mouth. The sensation was the same as before, he felt the touch as if she had taken him into her mouth. He sucked her, at first gently, and then harder, and he felt the spiral of desire run through her body until it culminated in the clenching of her thighs. He felt his own erection grow stiff.

"No," Spooky whimpered, pushing his head away from her breast. "It's my turn," she said when he pulled his head away in aroused astonishment.

"Your turn?" he asked, his senses screaming at him to strip her naked and push himself inside of her.

"Lay on your back," she ordered, breathing harshly. She sat up in the bed and pulled her bra off and tossed it to the floor. Her panties were quickly thrown in the same direction.

Balcher watched all of this with great appreciation, almost forgetting to rid himself of his own apparel. Which, incidentally, consisted only of the blue pair of briefs she'd bought him earlier in the day because, for some reason, she hadn't thought to buy him any pajamas. He pushed the briefs down his legs and kicked them off and then lay back on the bed as she had commanded him. His erection was full and proud and he saw her eyes gleam as she looked at him.

Spooky pushed the bed linens down to the foot of the bed and then she straddled Balcher's thighs. His hands reached out for her, but she grabbed him by the wrists and pushed them back over his head, the motion causing her stomach to come into contact with his shaft as she leaned over him. She felt that sensation deep in her groin. This communal sensation thing was amazing. She dearly hoped that this aspect of their connection would never fade, but if it did, she wanted to know exactly how it felt when she touched him... *and* when she took him in her mouth.

"Spooky?" he muttered, his voice hoarse as she held his hands over his head.

"No hands," she whispered, letting go of his wrists. She sat back on his thighs and watched as Balcher, with labored breaths, lowered his hands to grip both sides of his pillow case hard in his fists.

Then her eyes moved to his erection. His sex was big and pulsing, trembling with anticipation, the exact same anticipation she felt moments ago as she waited for his mouth to touch her breasts.

She reached an unsteady hand out for him, her nerve endings as heightened as his. She knew the first touch would cause a flinch of desire to sear her, just as it would him. Her fingertips touched his shaft and she gasped. A shiver went down her spine, settling in that place between her thighs, and she raised desire laden eyes to meet his and saw her own burning reflected in them. This slow seduction was so very sweet, and so very tormenting.

She looked back down at him at the exact moment he looked, their thoughts, emotions, and movements synchronized. She closed one hand around him and squeezed gently.

Ahh...that felt good.

Her head wanted to loll back, but she resisted because she wanted to see this. She moved her hand down his erection, the friction soft since he wasn't lubricated yet, and then back up.

Sweet! Oh, so sweet!

Dazed, she got up on her knees so that she could scoot back until she was straddling his shins. Then she leaned down, her elbows at the side of his hips to brace herself. She moved her face close to the head of his penis and breathed on him, her hot breath sending more shivers through her nerve endings. She heard him groan and felt the sound escape from her lips at the same time.

Unable to wait a second longer, she tasted him. The touch of her tongue rasped across the tip of his shaft and the sensation was overwhelming. Her thighs gripped the sides of his calves as she ground herself against him. Mindless, she took the whole head of his penis into her mouth and sucked hard, lashing him with her tongue as her hands stroked his shaft, massaging him up and down.

Balcher bucked against the pleasure, the immensity of it nearly taking his head off. The muscles of his arms bulged as he gripped his pillow case harder, her tongue doing things to him that he never before could have imagined. Then, when he could stand it no longer, he reached down and threaded his fingers through her hair on each side of her face as if he could control the hungry mouth that held him captive.

He felt her tongue find that place on the underside of the head of his penis that had always been so sensitive and he almost came. She felt it, too. Her body jerked against his shins as she rubbed her mound roughly against them. He heard her thoughts; she was almost growling in delirious satisfaction as her mouth, lips, and tongue knowingly did all the things guaranteed to take him higher.

He was flying, the pleasure almost painful and he wanted to let go and let it take him, but something was holding him back. Something on the back edge of his mind, which at the moment was nearly blinded by pleasure.

Then he remembered. With a hoarse cry, he pulled her mouth away from him.

"No," she whimpered, trying to get back to him, but he was too strong. He grabbed her under the arms and pulled her on top of him.

"Put me inside you," he ordered, his breathing harsh.

Spooky rose up and brought him to her opening. She sank down on him taking him deeper than ever before and the sensations caught hold again. The torturous burning took over her mind and she closed her eyes in ecstasy. Panting, she rode him, grinding her softness against Balcher's hips as they thrust up to meet her.

This was lightning, just like before, but better because she knew what it was and could enjoy the overwhelming pleasure without the fear that it would destroy her. Within moments, the splintering came, crashing through her again and again, and Spooky ground her teeth together in a guttural cry.

Balcher convulsed beneath her and the sensation of his seed shooting into her sent her over again. Her body gripped him, milking him as she gasped for breath.

Unlike before when it was over, she didn't pull away in exhaustion. She wanted to hold him inside her. She loved the way it felt to have him filling her opening and wedged tightly into the vee of her thighs against her mound. She lay down on his chest and held him as he fought the tremors that shook him from head to toe.

Eventually, as their breathing calmed, she murmured softly into his ear, "Why did you stop me? That felt so good!"

She felt his chest move. It was a low rumble of laughter.

"You clench your teeth when you come," he whispered.

Her brow puckered, and then she saw the light. Clenched teeth and fellatio don't go well together. "Ouch!" She chuckled.

"If this thing we have is permanent, then we'll have to watch out for that. I like my manhood just the way it is," he growled humorously and then he yawned.

She reached up and gave him a quick kiss on the lips. "I'll keep that in mind," she said, lassitude sinking in and causing her to yawn as well. With a small sigh of regret, she pulled her hips away from his, releasing him from her body, and then rolled onto her back beside him in exhaustion. They lay there silently, side by side, until their bodies cooled from their exertion and the air-conditioning became too much for Spooky. She sat up, grabbed the sheet from the foot of the bed, and pulled it up over them both before snuggling into his side. His arm went around her, holding her close.

"Go to sleep," she said sleepily. "Tomorrow's gonna be a difficult day. We'll need all the rest we can get."

The words were barely out of her mouth before sleep captured her.

She saw the underground garage and heard the screaming. Spooky ran towards the sound, her heart beating hard with fear and guilt. Shadows were everywhere, looming towards her like fingers of evil trying to grasp hold of her.

Her wall was up and she felt him trying to get though. She couldn't let him, he'd die! She winced as something like a hammer smashed into her mind. Her knees hit the cement floor of the parking garage and she almost screamed out in pain. She held the cry in, but it hurt so badly!

Oh, God! He was desperate. She heaved in an effort to get her breath without giving in to the need to cry. She wanted to answer him, to tell him to go away, that she could handle this, but she didn't dare let him in. He'd find her!

She felt the woman's fear again. It came at her in waves, clawing at her in desperation, and it forced her back onto her feet. She stumbled as she ran between the cars heading around the concrete wall for the fourth level.

She wanted to shout at her, to tell her to hold on, but the Ice Man would hear her. Her only chance to fix this was to blindside him and take him out. To do that, she would have to teleport, then come up behind him, grab him and then teleport again. Take him into nothingness and leave him there for all eternity.

She stopped abruptly, gagging with nausea at the thought of it. To start with, it might not work. But if it did, she would have him inside of her for the rest of her life. She would have that coldness, that evil sheathed in ice, infecting her mind and making her useless, or worse yet, dangerous to humanity for all time.

She would lose Balcher. She would lose everything.

She might as well be dead.

She decided right then and there to do what she'd read in that novel of Dean Koontz's. She would teleport, over and over again, until there was nothing left of either of them but a giant blob of flesh with no mind, no soul. That would be the end of it.

With that resolve to bolster her confidence, she put everything else out of her head and with a strong-willed determination, she pushed away from the car she was resting against and headed towards the sound of the woman's screams.

She was at the lower end of the parking garage's fourth level when she felt something crash through the wall of her mind. Her wall shattered, tumbling down as effortlessly as the walls of Jericho and she was defenseless to Balcher's invasion.

'You can't do this!' he shouted into her mind and she felt him. Oh, God! He was here! Somewhere close by!

'Stay out of this, Balcher!' she warned. She didn't dare put the wall back up. She needed to know where he was at all times.

'I love you, Spooky. We'll do this together. There's got to be another way!'

She felt him close and it shook her determination. 'I love you, too. That's why it has to end this way. Please, stay away. He's going to kill you!'

'Sarah...Sarah, sweetheart,' he whispered in her head, 'we can do this together. Please, listen to me. My path is clear. It's leading me to you. Remember? You trust that don't you?'

She faltered. He was telling the truth. She could see it in his mind.

He was meant to be here? Then why did she feel so strongly that he was going to die?

'I'm not going to die, Sarah. I promise you that. Wait for me.'

His words were like a warm blanket on a cold day, wrapping around her and making her feel safe. They made her want to believe him. Tears ran down her face in indecision.

She heard the woman scream again and almost simultaneously, she heard sirens in the distance. Someone must have called the police. Whatever she was going to do, she had to do it fast. She couldn't afford witnesses.

She couldn't afford to wait on Balcher, either. She edged out of the shadows between the cars and put herself right out in the open. She walked straight down the middle of the garage knowing that the Ice Man would see her coming. She was twenty feet closer to the *area where she felt the woman's fear concentrated when her worst nightmare came out from behind a van with his trembling captive.*

The Ice Man's right forearm was braced across the woman's throat, holding her tightly against his chest and in his right hand was his gun. It was his left hand, however, that held Spooky's attention. It held a knife and the blade was against the woman's jugular, bare millimeters from tearing her throat open.

She froze. Even if she could teleport and come up behind him, she might not be in time. And if he was holding onto the woman at the time, would she go with them? Spooky couldn't take that chance. She'd have to get him to let her go.

"I'm here," she said, holding her hands out to show she had no weapon. "Let her go."

Before he could answer, the sounds of footsteps alerted both of them to Balcher's arrival. Spooky turned in time to see Balcher point his gun at the Ice Man.

"Drop your weapon, Detective, or I'll slit this woman's throat," the Ice Man ordered.

Balcher eased up close to Spooky, and as he had before that day on the rooftop, he pushed her behind him. At the same time, Spooky felt his protectiveness close around her mind as well. Somehow, he was blocking her from what he was thinking.

He tossed his gun about ten feet away. "You can let her go now," he told the Ice Man.

It happened so fast that Spooky didn't see it coming. The Ice Man pulled the blade across the woman's throat, and blood gushed as she fell to the ground convulsing. At the same time, he pointed his gun at Balcher and pulled the trigger.

Time froze.

Spooky saw the bullet in mid-air, just inches from Balcher's chest, frozen in time as if she could just pluck it out of the air. The woman was on the ground ten feet away, her hand over her throat, the bright red blood spurting through her fingers, except it was frozen as well, like in a three-dimensional photograph, the droplets of blood hanging in the air like the bullet...

Spooky gasped and sat straight up in bed. She glanced apprehensively to her side and saw Balcher twitching in his sleep. She threw a wall up around her mind and he calmed down.

Oh, God. A vision. A premonition.

She was shaking uncontrollably. Balcher and that woman were going to die! And it was all because of her!

She threw the sheet off of her and scooted off the bed. Goose bumps covered her flesh as she paced naked through the darkness of the hotel room in horror.

She had to think! She could change this! She knew she could!

At least, she hoped she could. Out of the three visions she'd had before, the last one where Derek's plane crashed was the only one where she'd been able to change the outcome.

The first one, the one where she'd seen her mother's death, had been immutable. She taken her mother's stash of drugs and flushed them down the toilet. She'd even gotten her mother and her mother's drug dealer arrested by turning them both into the police with an anonymous call to 911. It didn't matter, her mother had still died.

And it happened exactly as she had foreseen it in her vision. She woke up that next morning, went to the front door to grab the Sunday newspaper left in the hallway and then headed for the kitchen to make coffee. She stopped in the doorway, confronted by the awful picture of her mother dead, slumped over the kitchen table with a rubber tube tied around her arm and a needle sticking out of her arm.

She just stood there, staring, not even truly shocked because there was something about the vision from the very first that had felt right. Well, not right, exactly. *True.* That's how it felt. Like it was meant to be.

Her mother should never have been let out of jail. It was one of those flukes where someone didn't do their job checking her history—an ex-con would have never been let out so easily. But the jail was overcrowded, so when the dealer posted bail for both of them, they were let out.

Meant to be.

Those words were sometimes comforting, sometimes painful.

Her second vision was just as concrete. She was working as a file clerk at an insurance company when she was twenty. At that time in her life, a job where she was essentially cloaked in isolation in the dusty basement of the establishment was the only kind of work she could do with any piece of mind. She'd tried being a waitress, but constant contact with the public was too chaotic, too painful.

She was filing an insurance claim for a woman who had just died from cancer when she caught a flash of a vision. She saw the woman's husband commit suicide. She thought that it was something that had already happened—premonitions were out of the ordinary except for that one of her mother—but the vision nagged at her until she got the nerve to call the home number on the file. A man answered and she knew immediately that she was speaking with the man in her vision. She heard the pain in his voice, his disinterest in life palpably coming to her over the phone, as if she could have been God calling and he wouldn't have cared. He wanted to be with his wife. That's all there was to it.

She replaced the receiver without a word. Nothing she could have said would have made a difference. She looked in the file for other dependants, but he was the only one listed. She hadn't really had to look because she saw no children in the man's life, no job worth living for, and no friends to help him through his grief. His wife's illness had been a long one, isolating them in their grief over the last ravaging months of her life.

She will never know if she could have changed the outcome of that vision because she never tried. She just waited day after day, hour by hour, until she saw his death announcement in the paper.

Her cowardice in confronting him shamed her. She told herself that she couldn't have changed his mind or his future—she hadn't helped her mother, had she?—so she didn't have anything to be ashamed of.

It didn't help.

So, when she saw that man from the casino die in a plane crash, she knew she had to try and change it if at all possible. The least she could do was to find the plane she saw in her vision and touch it. To her amazement, it worked. She changed a possible future. At least, she hoped she did. She never checked with Derek to see if that man took his intended flight. And since she never saw the guy again, she didn't know if he was still alive or not. He could have gotten hit by a bus or taken a jump out of a window for all she knew.

Death was concrete, wasn't it? Isn't that what the Bible says? A time to be born. A time to die?

Meant to be???

She stopped pacing the floor long enough to pick up her bra and panties from the floor where she'd thrown them. Then she went to the dresser and pulled out the rest of her clothes. She and Balcher hadn't stopped by her house for anything last night because the 'path' led them directly to the airport outside of town. All they had besides the clothes on their backs was her cell phone and the money she had grabbed before they left.

She pulled her clothes on and then put her cell phone in her pants pocket. She folded all of their remaining cash and stuck it into her other pants pocket. She couldn't leave him any of it or he'd find a way back to Las Vegas and get himself killed.

Still shaken, she went to the chair by the window and sat down in it, pulling her legs up underneath her. She needed to concentrate on her vision. She had to have the details clear in her mind.

One thing was clear. In her vision, she had known that Balcher was going to die. That's why she was there without him and had her wall up. Only the wall wasn't strong enough because he'd found a way to break through it. She would have to find another way to shield her mind. Something impenetrable.

Glass, like she'd used last night, wouldn't work. Steel would, though. A three-inch thick steel ball that encircled her mind completely. That would do the trick. She tried it. She closed her eyes and imagined the ball around her mind. When she opened her eyes, everything looked muffled. Sounded muffled, too. Even the humming of the air-conditioning unit was muted somewhat.

It frightened her. This would not only block Balcher from being able to see or hear her, it would also block her from being able to reach out with her mind. She needed to be able to do that or she would be helpless when she came up against the Ice Man.

She was at a loss at what to do. She needed something strong enough to keep Balcher out, but not so concrete that she couldn't venture out with her mind. Anything less and he would find a way to break through to her. She felt sure of that. He was a determined man.

And he loved her. She remembered that part of the vision with a heavy heart. He would not handle her death very well. He would be as lonely for the rest of his life as she had been throughout the first of hers.

She couldn't die. If at all possible, she had to come up with another way to handle the Ice Man, one that did not involve tripping with him. And she couldn't forget the woman in her vision, either.

She concentrated as hard as she could but could find no information about the woman in her memory. Neither did she recognize which parking garage she was in. Odds were in favor of it being a casino. Except that she did not see as many by-standers as she would have if it was a casino. People were coming and going at all times in those places and she couldn't ever remember being alone in a casino parking garage.

So, maybe it wasn't a casino. She frowned.

What other kinds of business's in Las Vegas were big enough to need a parking garage, but wouldn't have the foot traffic a casino has?

If it was an employee parking garage of some kind, it would not be that busy except in the morning, at lunch, and in the evenings when it was time to go home. A bank, maybe? Or some kind of industry? Radicom came to mind, but it didn't have a parking garage, just a parking lot.

It didn't help worrying about it. Outside of the casinos, she didn't know the Las Vegas business district all that well. She needed to find the man she came to Atlanta to find and get whatever information she could from him.

And she couldn't take Balcher with her.

Which brought her right back where she started. She had to find a way to block her mind from him. She liked the idea of steel. It gave the impression of great strength. She thought about that for a minute and then smiled. She wouldn't surround her mind with steel; she would imagine her mind being made of steel.

She closed her eyes. She could feel the change at first subtlety and then it strengthened. The mushy gray cells of her brain became the iron gray of steel. Her head even felt heavier to her as it rested on her shoulders. She opened her eyes and everything was clear. The hum of the air-conditioning was just as loud as before.

Now, to see if Balcher could hear her thoughts.

Balcher, wake up! The room's on fire!

Nothing. He didn't even wince in his sleep. She'd screamed those words so loud in her mind that he would have fallen out of the bed if he'd heard them.

One more test and she'd be home free. She went to the bathroom and after closing the door, she turned on the light. She looked around for something that neither of them had touched earlier that night. Her eyes fell on the hairdryer attached to the wall. She hadn't washed her hair earlier; she was afraid to do it so soon after her new dye job. Of course, Balcher had let his dry naturally.

She reached out and took the dryer out of its cradle and held it. She closed her eyes and concentrated hard. Seconds later her eyes popped open and she smiled. She'd seen the woman that used it this morning. She was getting ready to go for a job interview at Atlanta's new aquarium. It looked like a fantastic opportunity for a marine biologist and Spooky felt a momentary flash of jealousy at this view of a normal, but exciting, life.

She was excited. Her clairvoyance was working normally. She would just have to hope that everything else would work as well.

She turned off the light and snuck out of the bathroom quietly. Balcher was still asleep, in fact he was snoring slightly. The sight melted her for a moment, and then she hardened her heart. She had to do this without him no matter how pissed off he would be when he woke up to find her gone.

She squashed the desire to give him a quick kiss on the forehead—it would certainly wake him up—and then went out of the hotel room door, closing it gently behind her. She headed straight for the registration desk and paid their hotel bill for an entire week. Then she handed the clerk five hundred dollars.

"Put this on my account. It's to go for any room service ordered from my room. And make sure you tell my boyfriend, Michael Balcher, that it's there," she said to the clerk who was giving her a strange look. "Write his name down. I want to make sure you remember to tell him or he'll starve. Oh, and tell him that I'll be back in a few days to get him." She gave a stern look at the girl behind the counter. "One last thing. You are not—under no circumstances whatsoever—to give Balcher any of this money in cash. Only food. You got it? He'll waste it on drugs. I've put him here to dry out, if you know what I mean."

The girl behind the desk gave Spooky a big-eyed nod. "You can count on me," she said. "I'll make sure the other staff knows not to give it to him, either. If that's okay with you," she said quickly.

"Perfect," Spooky said. "He'll try all kinds of stories to make you give in and he's very convincing. The last time I tried this, he told them he was a cop from Las Vegas here on a case and that he had to get back immediately. Said it was a matter of life or death." She snorted and rolled her eyes. "Don't let him fool you."

"I won't," the girl said, crossing her heart.

Spooky almost smiled and ruined the effect. If the Ice Man didn't kill her, Balcher might try it himself after this.

"Can you call me a cab?" she asked the girl after thanking her for her assistance. It was nearly six o'clock in the morning, but Atlanta was a huge town. Their cab services should be 24/7.

At the girl's nod, she went out to the luggage drop off area to wait for her ride.

Chapter Thirteen

Balcher rolled over in bed. Sleeping felt so good, he didn't want to open his eyes. He reached out for Spooky, but she wasn't there. He frowned and then reluctantly forced his eyes open. He was alone in the bed.

He glanced at the clock on the bedside table and it read nine o'clock. He sat up and scratched his head. They were supposed to leave here by eight, weren't they? He looked around the room, the dimness dissipating as his eyes cleared. Spooky wasn't anywhere in the room.

He put his feet on the floor. She was probably in the bathroom. Her moving around was likely what woke him up. He sat there a few minutes and then picked up the TV remote on the table. He would check to see what was happening in Atlanta, Georgia on this fine morning while he waited for her to come out of the bathroom.

Five minutes passed and she was still in the bathroom. He couldn't hear her thoughts, either. He became alarmed. He got up off of the bed and went to stand by the bathroom door.

"Spooky," he yelled through the door.

Nothing.

He opened the door and peeked inside. She was not there.

Then his stomach growled and a reason for her disappearance occurred to him. He smiled. She was out somewhere getting them breakfast. He closed his mind and concentrated to see if he could touch her mind from a distance like he did before.

The smile left his face. All he could see was gray—iron gray.

Now that was weird.

Getting spooked—no pun intended—he went to put his clothes on. After dressing, he checked the dresser for her clothes. They were gone as he expected. All of their money was gone, too. That he did not expect.

Spooky!

He sent her name out into the atmosphere hoping that she would respond to him from wherever she was. It was like yelling into a canyon; all he heard was the echo of his own voice coming back at him.

The hairs on the back of his neck stood up, but this time he could tell it was not from being near her. He called down to the front desk and got the operator. "Yes, can you tell me if anyone left a message for room number 225?"

He waited for a few minutes and then someone different came on the line. "Is this Mr. Michael Balcher?" the voice asked.

"Yes," he answered, gripping the phone hard in his hand. If they knew his name, then something was definitely up.

"Mr. Balcher, my name is David Childers. I'm the manager of this hotel. Ms. Knight left a message that she would be back in a few days to get you. She said not to worry; she's paid for the room till the end of the week and left us funds for room service for whenever you get hungry."

Balcher gripped the phone hard as his gut twisted in fear and betrayal.

Dammit! What the hell was she thinking!

He nearly threw the phone at the wall before he recovered himself enough to speak politely into the phone. "Listen, Mr. whoever the hell you are. I am a police detective with the Las Vegas Police Department. I need you to send those funds up to my room immediately. I'm checking out," he growled.

"I'm sorry, Mr. Balcher. Ms. Knight told us you'd say that. We're aware of your drug problem. My clerk took Ms. Knight's instructions to keep the money away from you, but she did so without my permission. As manager of this hotel, I won't have any shenanigans going on in my hotel. I can't give you the money, but if you want to leave, that's up to you. If you choose to stay, you'd better be on your best behavior or I'll have the police here to take care of you. Is that clear?" the man asked snottily.

"As a bell," Balcher spit out as he slammed the phone down. "Damn you, Spooky," he snarled to the empty hotel room. He grabbed the phone back up and tried to place a long distance call out. It wouldn't work. She must have barred all outside calls from this phone. He slammed it back down again. Oh, he was truly pissed!

He paced the room, thinking furiously. Why did she do this? He racked his brain for a clue as to what was going on in her mind, but he couldn't find anything. He didn't see this coming, at all. How could she have hidden this from him?

He threw himself into the chair by the window and jerked as the contact with the cushions thrust a flash of a vision into his mind.

Parking garage. Woman bleeding. Gray metal.

What the hell was that? He wondered, shakily. He closed his eyes and tried to get more, but all he could see was that damned gray metal. It was everywhere.

"Parking garage, woman bleeding, gray metal," he said aloud, hoping the words would mean something. He frowned. They did seem familiar, especially the first two images. They danced at the edge of his consciousness, not close enough to be clear. He laid back in the chair and closed his eyes again. He didn't try to get another vision from the chair, because like Spooky said before, it wouldn't do him any good. He just cleared his mind of all thoughts and waited for something to come to him.

He sat there for a long while and then let the image of a parking garage come into his mind. He didn't push the image, he just let it settle there and he saw himself walking through it.

Stay out of this, Balcher!

The words came to him as if in a dream. He jerked and sat up a little straighter, but he let his mind continue to wander.

I love you, Spooky. We'll do this together. There's got to be another way!

He heard his answer to her. In his mind, he could feel his terror at what she was going to do. It was suicide.

I love you, too. That's why it has to end this way. Please, stay away. He's going to kill you!

Balcher opened his eyes. He remembered his dream, only it wasn't a dream, it was real. He went to the bed and sat down to make an inside call. He ordered room service, and lots of it. While he waited on the food, he took another shower. He would be back in Las Vegas by this evening. If Spooky thought she could stop him, she didn't know him as well as she thought she did!

Room service came. He answered the knock, allowing the server to push the cart inside. His expression nearly frightened the poor girl out of her wits.

He devoured the food, having no enjoyment in the sustenance as its only purpose was to fuel him for the day ahead.

He pushed the cart outside into the hall and with the hotel's card key in his pocket, he left the room, looking for a pay phone.

Outside the entrance to the hotel, he scanned all the roads available to him looking for the clarity he remembered from yesterday. One way, in particular, stood out. It was practically vibrating. He set out walking and had covered at least two miles before he found a pay phone. He didn't have a quarter, but he didn't need one. All he had to do was to follow the instructions for a collect call on the panel using his precinct's direct number. Meyers, the desk sergeant, took the call, and after giving him heck about losing his wallet—Zack must have opened his big mouth—he put him through to his annoying partner.

"Mikey, long time no hear," Zack said at the other end of the line. "You still hugging the toilet—"

"Shut up, Zack, and listen," he said with aggravation. "Did you find my wallet?"

"My, my, aren't we in a snit—"

"Zack," Balcher said, threateningly.

"Okay! You don't have to take my head off," his partner said with a pout Balcher could nearly see over the phone. "Yeah, I got your wallet. I left you a message on your answering machine, you big dolt. If you'd just—"

Balcher cut him off again. "I'm not at home, Zack. I'm in Atlanta. I don't have any money or I.D. and I've got to get back to Vegas as soon as possible."

"What the hell are you doing in Atlanta?"

"I don't have time to explain it all to you, right now," Balcher growled. "Listen, you've got to call the Atlanta airport and get me a plane ticket back to Vegas. Use one of my credit cards to pay for it, and then either fax them or email them a copy of my driver's license and police I.D. Tell them it's a police emergency. And then I want you to call this number," he read a phone number off of a sign for the car rental agency across the street, "...and use the same credit card to rent a car for me."

"Mikey—"

"Just do it, Zack And then call me back on this pay phone," he looked down to find the number displayed crookedly above the cradle for the handset and read it aloud. "Let me know when it's done. I'll be waiting," Balcher said and then hung up the phone before Zack could ask any more questions.

He stood there on the hot pavement of the parking lot with the sun baking down on his head and the humidity of the day nearly searing his lungs. He was furious.

And he was scared. If the Ice Man got to Spooky before he got back, she wouldn't have a chance.

He spotted a bench nearby and settled there to wait.

Chapter Fourteen

Spooky left the man's office with only one item of useful information. It was a name, Nicholas Brandson. The same name the guy used at the casino in Las Vegas when he was trying to draw her out.

He was bold, she'd have to give him that. Either that or he had several aliases that he used and he was sticking to this one for now.

She had contacts. If he was staying in any of the casinos under this name, she would find him. She pulled her cell phone out of her pocket and called Harrell on his private line at the casino. She may as well start there and, if she talked to him nice enough, he might be willing to do some of the leg work for her.

"Hi, it's me, Spooky," she said when he picked up. "I wondered if you could do me a favor?" She could almost see his response as he considered his answer. He would be lying back in that expensive leather swivel chair of his with a smug expression on his face and wondering what he could ask of her in return.

"It'll cost you," he said finally. "Five thousand."

She never expected him to ask for money. "I'll write you a check—"

"That's not what I meant," he said, correcting her. "I meant your fee. In the future, when I need you, it'll cost me five grand, not twenty."

"If I charge you five grand, then everybody else will want to get in on the action," she hedged. "Ten grand and it's a deal." She waited while he calculated that figure in his head. The guy was practically an adding machine in clothes.

"All right, make it ten," he agreed. "What do you want from me?"

"Information. Remember that Nicholas Brandson guy from the other day?"

"Yeah. What about him?"

She heard the interest in his tone. He was going to do this for her, she could feel it. "I need to know where he's staying while he's in town. Can you check around and then get back to me on my cell when you find him?"

"Well, isn't this an interesting development. The psychic needs my help to find someone," he said gleefully.

It was the first time that he openly called her a psychic. Well, she'd pretty much given that away the last time she saw him. "Rub it in, why don't you?" she muttered, more to give him the enjoyment of having her in his pocket than anything else. Harrell liked having people owe him.

"There's not something wrong, is there? I mean, you still have those hocus pocus, voodoo powers of yours, don't you?" he asked, sounding a bit worried. She was a precious commodity to him and he wanted her in full working order.

"I'm still the same, if that's what you're asking. But this guy's a ghost. I can't seem to hone in on him, if you get my drift."

"You do it by touch, don't you? I knew it," he said excitedly. "Without anything of this guy's to touch, you can't perform your magic."

"If you say so," she said mysteriously, not willing to give him all her secrets. "Of course, if you tell anybody these crazy ideas you have about me, they'll think you're nuts."

"I wouldn't bet on that if I were you, Spooky. Rumors have been floating around about you since you started making your casino rounds. We—those of us that have been paying your exorbitant fees for the past few years—have a bet going with sixty/forty odds that you are, in fact, psychic. The day I prove it, I'll be a wealthy man."

"You're already a wealthy man," she said half-heartedly. Their conversation was making her ill. All this time, she'd thought she was being inconspicuous. How naïve could she be?

"You can never be wealthy enough." He laughed. "So, if I find your fella, what are you gonna do with him?"

Spooky hesitated for a moment and then said, "Don't be surprised to find either him or me dead in a parking garage, somewhere." She needed to get this issue out of the way right now because if her vision was real, that was essentially what was going to happen. She wanted to know beforehand how Harrell was going to react when it did. Besides, Winston Harrell was not totally clean himself, and he had some rather disreputable connections. After all, this was Las Vegas.

As long as he was forewarned that this guy would turn up dead, she was pretty sure that he'd keep his nose out of it and he would be appreciative of the fact that she had warned him ahead of time.

"It had better not be you, Spooky," he said and then he hung up.

She had her answer. It was a good thing she lived in Vegas. What happens in Vegas, stays in Vegas, wasn't that the catch phrase? Casinos ran the town, and that meant that casino operators ran the town. All in all, she felt secure that he would cover her back.

She made a second call. "Derek, I'll be at the airport in an hour. Be ready to fly." She listened for a moment and then answered. "Nope. Just me. My friend has decided to stay in Atlanta." She flipped the two sides of her phone together and then gave the cabbie that she had paid well to stay with her all morning the address of the airport.

She was finally headed home.

Derek flew her safely into Las Vegas. Spooky picked up the rental car they'd left outside of the hangar last night and headed for the casino to speak with Harrell in person.

When she got to the casino, she saw that the 'path' was clear to the parking area where she'd parked her car so she headed in that direction and found an open parking space right next to her vehicle. That was a pretty clear omen, now wasn't it?

Using the key she'd hidden on the backside of the tag on the front of her car, she let herself into the driver's side door and then reached under the dashboard and into her special compartment to get her driver's license and a credit card.

That done, she headed for the casino. It felt really comfortable to be home even though she knew that the next couple of days would be dangerous for her. She was thankful that Balcher was still in Atlanta. At least, her biggest worry was out of the way.

She couldn't help smiling as she thought of him. He was going to be incredibly angry with her, that's for sure, but he'd get over it. If the plan that she'd come up with on the plane ride back into town worked, they'd have plenty of time to sort out their problems later.

She refused to consider the possibility that her vision could not be changed. Balcher was not going to be killed by a bullet in that parking garage. Of course, she was pulled out of the vision before it was finished, but even if he had been shot, she supposed that she would have jumped on him and teleported them out of there like she did before.

Her vision did not necessarily mean that Balcher was going to die, but it could mean that the woman was going to die. There was no way she could have saved both of them.

She frowned. It was incredible to her that she would have been given this gift of precognition, of seeing the future, if there was not something she could do about what she saw. She hadn't helped her mother, of course, and she had surely wracked her brains over the years to figure out exactly what she did wrong there.

Maybe she should have told her mother what she saw? No. That wouldn't have worked. She knew that the moment she thought it. It was like that man whose wife died from cancer that she saw committing suicide; his death was inevitable because he wanted to die. It's taken her until now to realize that her mother wanted death just as fervently as that man had. Nothing could have helped her.

But the man she saw die in the plane crash must surely be alive because Derek was. She frowned. No, that wasn't necessarily so, either. Even if she hadn't interfered and found what was wrong with Derek's plane that day, he may have survived the crash when it happened. Her vision of the crash site that day showed a plane that was mostly intact, just bent up and sitting askew, its tail section—where the passenger sat bleeding—bent around a tree trunk.

Passenger sat bleeding...

She scrunched up her brow. Maybe he hadn't been dead after all. Maybe he'd just been injured and would have made it out of that wreck alive.

A chill went down her spine. If that was so, then maybe death was concrete. Maybe there was an appointed time for everyone to die, and nothing anybody could do would ever be able to change it.

She took a deep breath. She had not actually seen Balcher die, nor that other woman. The vision ended with their fates literally frozen in time.

She entered the casino and the ghostly, mixed echoes of sorrows and a few joys surrounded her mingling with her own fears and nearly dragging her down. She determinedly shrugged them off and then approached a security guard to ask him to let Harrell know she was there. Then she headed for the elevators to wait for him to come down to the casino floor.

Moments later, he stepped out of an elevator and she moved to intercept him. He paused to keep from running into her and then, after a brief look at her face and a dismissive but polite nod, he stepped around her to head into the casino.

"Harrell?" she asked, bewildered by his dismissal.

He stopped and turned around. He gave her a second glance and then a look of recognition came over his face, followed closely by a look of astonishment.

"Spooky?" he asked.

"Fat injections, a hair cut and dye job," she muttered. "Don't ask," she said, trying to quickly shrug off the subject. "I just came by to see if you've heard anything yet."

"You look really good!" Harrell said appreciatively.

Spooky blushed. This was the first compliment, besides Balcher's, that she'd gotten. She was not used to it. "Thanks," she said self-consciously.

"Let's go back up to the control room. I've got my eye on another card counter," he said, leading her back to the same elevator he just arrived in. They got in, he put his key in, and they headed for the fifth floor.

In the control room, he headed for the monitors and she followed him. "So, are you gonna tell me what you know?" Although he had ignored her question earlier, Spooky felt the confidence oozing from him. He'd definitely found something.

"Maybe. After you get this guy off my back, I might be able to think clearer," he said, giving her a knowing look and pointing to a guy on his monitor.

She rolled her eyes. "I'll be right back." She held out her hand for his key to the elevator.

He gave it to her and smiled brightly.

Spooky went into the elevator and down to the floor of the casino. She walked up to the guy in question and placed her hand on his shoulder. "You need a kiss for good luck?" she murmured huskily. Something about Harrell's look earlier made her feel sexy and she couldn't resist trying her wiles out on the guy. Not that she'd consider anybody but Balcher as a lover, but if felt kind of good knowing that other men might find her attractive as well.

She got her flash even before the guy had time to look over his shoulder. He was definitely counting cards and he'd nearly been caught doing it at the Venetian last week.

His muscles tightened under her hand, and then he finally turned and gave her a weak smile. "Maybe next time, honey. I'm finished here," he said, grabbing his chips from the table and taking off.

Spooky was surprised. Somehow, just from her hand on his shoulder, he knew he'd been caught. Funny, she hadn't detected any psychic abilities from him. She shrugged and headed back to Harrell.

"Great! You scared him off!" Harrell growled as soon as she stepped out of the elevator.

"How'd I do that?" she asked.

"You touched him. He thought you were casino personnel coming to warn him off. Why'd you touch him? You've never done that before."

"Because it was the quickest way to see what he was up to," she said with a frown. "I didn't come in here today to catch card sharps. I need to find Nicholas Brandson!"

He gave her a hard look. "Are you sure you're really Spooky?" he asked.

She frowned. "What do you mean?"

"You kinda look like her, but then again, you don't. And you sure as hell ain't acting like her."

"I've had a rough couple of days, if you don't mind," she said abruptly. "Having your life on the line has a way of changing people."

"In my office," Harrell ordered, motioning for her to follow him.

He closed the door and then sat behind his desk with a hand motion indicating that she should take a seat in the chair opposite him.

"I can take care of this problem for you," he offered, eyeing her seriously.

Spooky's eyebrows went up. She knew he had connections, but she never dreamed they went as far as this. Of course, he would never expose himself by saying the actual words, but Spooky was pretty sure he just offered to have Brandson killed for her. It was an appealing idea and she considered it for a moment. Then she shook her head to the negative.

"I have to do this myself," she said. "He has information that only I could get from him, if you know what I mean. But I appreciate the offer. I just need his location."

"What about after?" he asked.

"You're asking how I intend to dispose of the...um...trash?" she asked with a half-smile.

He nodded.

"I don't. I intend to let the authorities take care of that."

He frowned and Spooky figured that this was not exactly what he had expected to hear from her.

"I have the best lawyers in town, hell, the best lawyers in the country if you find yourself needing one," he offered.

She shrugged and gave him stare for stare. "I won't need one."

He frowned at her for the longest time, but then a smile broke out on his face. "You're a cool one, I'll give you that. You just remember who your friends are." He reached into his desk drawer and gave her an envelope. "Here's your guy."

He hopped up from his desk and led her to the door. Harrell didn't have the gene for lingering. He was an action kind of guy. "Happy hunting," he said in dismissal on his way out to watch the monitors at the other end of the control room.

Spooky found a security guard at her elbow. She shoved the envelope Harrell gave her into her pocket and then handed the guard the elevator key. This was standard procedure. Nobody got out of the casino with that key. Then she got onto the elevator with the guard to go to the ground floor. Although she was tempted, she didn't take a look at the contents of the envelope until she was sitting in her rental car waiting for the air-conditioning to kick in.

She'd considered taking her own car when she reached the area where both cars were parked, but the rental car was clearer and shimmering a bit. She suspected that her car might be known to Brandson at this point, and there was no reason to give him a heads-up that she was coming for him.

She opened the envelope and saw her destination. She was taken aback at the information and was seriously surprised by the audacity of the guy.

He was here. Brandson was in the hotel!

Oh, God! She was no where near being ready for him. She put the rental car in gear and hurriedly drove out of the parking lot. If Brandson was in his hotel room watching her car and waiting for her to show up, then he'd probably just gotten a good look at her earlier when she went into her car for her license.

Funny, she hadn't felt him watching her. Maybe he'd taken that exact moment to go to the door for room service or to go to the bathroom. Or it was possible that he didn't know what her car looked like and was just waiting at the hotel for her to come to him. He had to know she'd show up sooner or later!

She needed time to think this through. And she had a few things she needed to buy before she confronted him.

Before this day was over, she was determined that this thing was going to be settled once and for all.

Chapter Fifteen

Balcher waited at the baggage carousel for Zack to come find him and he was severely dreading the confrontation. He had practiced his explanation for his change in appearance several times in his head, but even he didn't believe the crap he'd come up with. Still, Zack wasn't the sharpest knife in the drawer, so maybe he'd get by with the nonsense.

He'd managed to convince those yoyos at the Atlanta airport that he was who he said he was, but that was different. His license was two years old; he could have lost weight and grown his hair in that long of a time frame, and his face was essentially the same.

This kind of a change in forty-eight hours, though, was going to be tougher, if not impossible, to explain. He glanced around the crowded baggage claim area for the umpteenth time and his eyes finally found their target. Zack was heading straight for him.

Maybe it wouldn't be that tough since Zack had apparently recognized him already. He smiled as Zack approached, then realized that Zack wasn't looking at him, but at some guy about fifty yards away. He growled, "Zack!"

Zack's head swung around until he found the source of the voice.

"Who the hell are you!" he asked belligerently, and then his mouth fell open. "Mikey!"

"Shut your trap, you'll catch flies!" Balcher snapped.

Zack looked him up and down in amazement. "What the hell happened to you?" he asked.

"Liposuction and a hair transplant," Balcher said, his words clipped. He had a long, drawn out explanation planned, but ten seconds in Zack's presence and he'd lost the patience to deliver it.

"They do all that to you in Atlanta?" Zack asked, bewildered. "Wow. Turn around. I can't believe it! Shouldn't you still be in a hospital or something? That must have hurt like hell. Bend over. I want to check out your scalp!"

Balcher took a deep breath and counted to ten. "Where's my wallet?" he asked between clenched teeth.

"What?"

"My...wallet," he ground out.

"Oh, here it is," Zack said, pulling the wallet out of his back pocket. "Oh, and your service weapon's in my car. I didn't mention that part to the captain, Mikey. He wouldn't have liked it that one of his detectives was so careless with his gun," Zack said, still looking Balcher over in amazement. "I bet all that work cost you a pretty penny, didn't it? I wonder how much they would charge for a nose job?"

Balcher ignored him and headed out of the airport. Zack practically had to skip to catch up to him. "Where'd you park?" Balcher barked.

"In the parking garage," Zack said, pointing to the structure across the road from the main entrance. "Fourth level," he said and then headed across the drive, dodging taxis and limousines.

Balcher stopped in his tracks. Zack's words just jiggled his memory. He remembered a sign in the parking garage from the vision. It had said 'LEVEL 4'. He was sure of it. He started moving again, catching up with Zack on the other side of the drive as he was about to enter the parking garage. Could this be where it all happens? He didn't remember Zack being in the vision so he was pretty sure it wouldn't be happening now. Still, it might not be a bad idea to check the garage out and see if anything looked familiar.

Instead of heading for the elevator like Zack, he walked out into the parking area. He was half way up the first level when Zack came jogging up behind him.

"Hey, Mikey, what're you doin'? They have elevators, you know?"

"Just checking something out," he answered. He looked around the structure, but couldn't be sure if it looked familiar or not. The danged places all looked alike. For one thing, the light was not right. It was darker, like maybe twilight, in the vision. It was barely after six, now. The sun wouldn't be setting for another three hours.

He headed up to the second level, then the third, and then the fourth. He was getting nothing. So, it wasn't the airport parking garage.

The immensity of the problem suddenly hit him. Vegas was full of parking garages. How the hell was he supposed to know which one it was?

He spotted Zack's red Honda and headed for it.

"You sure are acting strange, my friend. Like in one of those alien movies, uh, *The Body Snatchers*. Yeah, that's it!" he said, clicking his key chain remote to unlock his doors. "Some alien has taken your DNA and made a copy of you, only he forgot to make you fat and bald."

Balcher gave him an irritated look and then folded himself into Zack's tiny front passenger seat. "I was not bald; it was a crew cut," he said, pushing the seat back as far as it would go. It didn't help much. His head was still scraping the roof of the car and his knees were jammed against the dashboard. He felt like a freaking pretzel.

"Did they find my cars keys when they found my wallet?" he asked before Zack could make any more irritating remarks.

"Don't know. You didn't tell me to ask them for your keys," Zack answered. Then pointing to the glove compartment, he said, "Your weapon's in there."

Balcher had to contort into a strange position to open the glove compartment and get his weapon. "You'd think that if they had the presence of mind to give you my service weapon along with my wallet, that they'd have also given you my keys." He tucked his weapon into his waistband and then rearranged his knees again.

Zack frowned. "They also had some bloody clothes that they said they found with your stuff. I told them that it wasn't yours since you'd just called me and didn't mention any blood. Besides, if you didn't have your driver's license or car keys, then how the hell did you end up in Atlanta?"

Balcher was not surprised that his friend's detective instincts were finally kicking in. Although, it had taken longer than he thought it would. "A friend flew me out there."

"And you didn't have time to come by and get your wallet and gun from me? What the hell's going on, Mikey?" Zack asked.

"I was already on my way to Atlanta when I called you about that," Balcher lied. "I was nervous about the, uh, medical procedures, so I wasn't thinking straight."

"You're lying your ass off—what's left of it, that is—and I want to know why?" Zack said, his tone serious.

Balcher took a deep breath. "You wouldn't believe me if I told you, my friend. So, if you don't mind, let's save the explanations for later. I need to get to the casino and see if they have my car keys. My car's already there, so you can just drop me off."

"That's all you're gonna tell me, ain't it? You're just gonna leave me hanging?"

"For now, yeah. There's something I have to do tonight, but I'll call you as soon as I can." He returned Zack's skeptical stare and realized how much his old friend meant to him. If he told Zack about the danger he would soon be in, the guy would stick to him like a cocklebur. He couldn't afford to get him involved.

They arrived at the casino and Zack—still in a worried huff—dropped him off at the entrance. Balcher went in to the front desk of the hotel and asked if any keys had been turned in over the last couple of days.

"Any distinguishing items on your key ring," the female clerk asked him with a bright smile.

Balcher knew the expression was part of her job, but her perkiness got on his nerves, anyway. "Yeah...*keys*," he said sarcastically. He didn't go in for fancy doodads on his key ring. It was hard enough to keep up with all the keys he had.

"Ford, Chevrolet, Honda?" the clerk asked, her smile holding on by a toe nail, with only the slight clench of her teeth letting Balcher know he'd pissed her off.

"Ford Explorer. Seven keys on the key ring," he offered, stifling his impatience.

"Just a moment, sir," she said and then went through a door into an office. It was several minutes before she came back. A manager was with her.

"My name is Sherry Mathews. I am a manager—"

"What the hell is it, now?" he growled, remembering his conversation over the phone with a manager at that hotel in Atlanta. He sure as hell didn't want to go through that again.

She frowned. "I'm sorry, sir. It's just that we found a set of keys that matches your description, but I have to alert the police that you're here to retrieve them—"

Balcher pulled out his badge. "I am the police, ma'am. Now if you'll give me those keys?" he said, holding out his hand.

"I don't know," she hedged, looking his badge over. "I was told to call them if anyone came in for these keys. They were found in a pair of pants in the parking lot along with a shirt that was covered in blood. If you'll just wait until I call them?" she asked politely.

There was no way around it. Casinos were notorious for playing by the book. They policed themselves so thoroughly that it was almost unnecessary for the real cops to ever step foot in one of the places. If, on the off chance they did call for a real cop, the perps were usually surrounded by an army of security guards and already subdued and waiting on them.

He grunted, "Tell them Detective Balcher is here to pick them up."

He heard the manager talking with Meyers, the desk sergeant. Twice in one day the guy was getting a call from or about him. He was never gonna live this down!

Meyers must have confirmed his status as a police officer because the manager nodded at Balcher as she hung up the phone. "I'll be right back, Detective Balcher," the manager said and headed back to her office.

Balcher tapped his fingers impatiently on the wood of the desk as he waited, and the sound appeared to be making the clerk nervous as she attempted to assist the next person in line. Well, that was just too danged bad.

He took his eyes off of the girl and idly glanced around the joint. The hotel reservation desk was a whole lot quieter than the casino area and he was just killing time, but then something white caught his eye. He jerked around. About twenty yards away, the Ice Man stepped off of the escalator and then turned into the corridor that led to the casino.

The manager was just coming out of her office with his keys. He snatched them out of her hand with a terse 'thank you' and then ran towards the corridor to follow the guy. He was just in time to see him head into the casino. He followed him again, keeping that white hair within sight as the Ice Man threaded himself through the crowd and headed for the blackjack tables.

This was how he lured Spooky out the first time. Playing blackjack.

Balcher smiled. Harrell would call Spooky and she'd come running. All he had to do was watch and wait. And he'd thought that this was going to be hard!

A flash from Spooky's vision crossed his mind suddenly and his smile disappeared. He was right to begin with; this was going to be hard. It was going to damned hard.

Chapter Sixteen

Spooky came out of the sporting goods store with exactly what she had been looking for. She took her purchase out of the bag and laid it on the passenger seat. Her whole plan balanced on whether or not she was going to be able to take an inanimate object through the lights with her.

Balcher seemed to think she could. She wished she could lower her defenses and see what he was thinking right now, but she couldn't. He would distract her, even all the way from Atlanta.

She headed back to the casino and parked her rental car on the fourth level. She still wasn't certain that her vision took place at the casino's parking garage, but she had to check it out anyway. One thing was for certain, the time was later than this. In her vision the garage had been a lot darker, shadows everywhere. She looked at her watch. It was seven-thirty.

She got out of her car and walked around the area, hoping to get a vibe from something. She was nearly at the elevator when her cell phone rang.

"Spooky Knight," she answered.

"Harrell here. I've got your man playing at one of my blackjack tables. He's not winning big. I think he's just wasting time waiting on you to show up."

Spooky's insides quivered in sudden dread. This wasn't right. She looked around the parking garage. There were at least ten people that she could see from where she was at the elevator. Even one was too many. Plus, the time couldn't be right. It was too light in the garage. If she was calculating correctly, it would be closer to nine-thirty before it all happened.

Maybe this was her chance to change things! If she could lure him somewhere safe, she could try out her plan and then Balcher and that woman from her vision would be out of danger.

"I'm going to need your help with a few things," she finally said. "You're not going to like this, but I need for you to immediately block off the parking garage from arriving traffic. Then, once that's done, wait a couple of minutes and then get one of your security guards to pass Brandson a message to meet me in the garage on the fourth level. After he gets on the elevator, I need your guards to close off the parking garage elevators for about ten minutes. I don't need any witnesses if I can help it."

"This is crazy, Spooky! You can't be serious. I'm not going to help you take this guy out in my casino."

"If you don't help me, I'll just go to your blackjack table and bring him out here myself," she stated. "It's your patrons that will be in danger if they're not kept out of the way."

There was silence on the line for a moment. "Why does it have to be there on the fourth level?" he asked, angry and mystified.

"Because certain things are meant to be. This is one of them." As Spooky watched, shadows began to move stealthily between the cars, making the already dim garage turn eerily dark. It was as if the sun had suddenly gone behind a cloud, but she looked out towards the outer edge of the garage at the sky and nothing looked different.

She looked back. The shadows were filling the entire area. "You don't have a choice at this point, Harrell. It's happening already." Her voice was stoic, resolute.

"What's happening?" he practically screamed into the phone.

"Just get him out here. It has to be now. Do it!" She hit the end button and then held it down until the device cut off. She shoved it into her pocket. Harrell would do as she asked; he couldn't afford not to.

She looked around her and the shadows grew more sinister, as if she could see evil things moving around in them. Cold shivers went down her spine.

She headed back to her car at the lower end of the fourth level parking deck and opened the door. She threw her cell phone and car keys into the front seat and then grabbed the case from the passenger side. It was a small wooden case hinged on one side and had no lock. She opened it and saw the gleaming metal of the switchblade knife she'd just bought. She took it out of the case and holding it firmly in her hand, she pressed the button like she'd practiced at the sporting goods store. The blade shot out, the edges thin and sharp.

When she told the salesman what she needed, he assured her it was fine for cutting up deer. Although, he did look skeptical at her choice of knives since he had plenty of other choices more suitable. Now, with the time nearing that she'd be forced to use it, she found herself fervently hoping that the human chest was not any more resilient than that of a deer. She pressed the release and the blade went back into hiding.

Perfect.

She looked around the garage saw that it was empty and silent. She hadn't heard a car arrive in several minutes. Thankfully, people who come to casinos are in a hurry to get to their gambling and don't hang about at their cars.

Her plan was simple. With the knife securely in her hand, she'd trip to a spot right behind the Ice Man and then insert—*that term was preferable over the word stab*—the blade between his ribs and into his heart. If things went as planned, she'd then touch his dying body and get a vision of all the people he'd told about her. She hoped that since she was the main thing on Brandson's mind at the moment, that information would be right out there for her to see without her having to probe any deeper. She was extremely reluctant to forge any kind of a deeper connection with him.

The biggest crimp in her plan, of course, was the pain she always felt coming out of a trip. Somehow, she'd have to control it long enough to stab him. She was stronger now, thanks to Balcher, so she was determined that she would carry this plan off without a hitch.

She was about to shut the car door when she heard footsteps. She glanced apprehensively around and saw a woman fifty yards ahead of her heading for the elevator.

Where did she come from?

Spooky shut her car door softly and stumbled out into the middle of the garage so that she could see the woman better.

Oh, God! It was the woman from her vision!

The woman had long black hair and was wearing a green blouse and black pants...exactly like in her vision. Spooky tried to call out to her to run, but her throat had closed up in fear. She knew genuine fear now. Petrified fear.

This was not the way it was supposed to happen! She'd changed things, hadn't she?

The woman, whose face was lit from the lights near the elevator, was reaching out to touch the elevator's call button. Before she could push it, the door opened suddenly.

Spooky finally found her voice. "No!" she screamed. "Run! Get back to your car!"

The woman turned, her hair flying around her shoulders as she moved cautiously away from the elevator.

Spooky felt her indecision even from a distance. She pushed her mind out as far as she could to try and connect with her. When she did, she got a few general impressions of the woman. She was the kind of woman that would help a stranger in distress, but she was also a woman who'd known great fear. She was being torn between trying to see who it was that was screaming at her, and her instinct to run, to get into the elevator and escape the horrible thing that was happening in the darkness. She looked scared, her fear emblazoned on her face as she scanned the shadows surrounding her.

"Get away from the elevator! Run!" Spooky shouted again, her voice hoarse as she made her trembling legs carry her towards the woman.

She was too late.

*   *   *

Balcher followed the Ice Man from the Blackjack tables to the end of the casino where the parking garage elevators were. He watched the man get in the elevator and was about to punch the button for the other elevator when security guards flooded the area.

"Stand aside," one of the guards yelled at him.

Balcher hadn't expected this. He stumbled back, glancing around him for an opening. The stairwell door gleamed at him.

The path!

He didn't hesitate, he ran for the stairwell. In his flight, he realized what was happening. Spooky, through her connection with Harrell, was blocking all the exits. She wasn't taking any chances that someone else would get hurt.

Just as soon as he was through the stairwell door, he came face to face with another two guards. They were blocking access to the stairs going up, but they didn't have the door to the first level of the parking garage blocked. He ran at that door, pushed it open and raced out into the parking deck.

Fourth level! He had four decks to go up!

He ran through structure dodging cars as he went and his heart was racing with fear. He remembered the vision and what Spooky was thinking of doing. She was going to commit suicide and take that bastard with her. He had to get to her before that happened! He was coming fast around the second level when he heard a woman scream.

*   *   *

Brandson came out of the elevator and grabbed the woman around the neck. The woman screamed, pure terror distorting her features. Her hands grabbed at the muscular arm encircling her throat, but he was too strong. Brandson had her half off of her feet, holding her as easily as if she was a large doll.

"Spooky!" he yelled, turning one way, then the other looking for her.

Spooky tried to sink down into the shadows of a nearby car. She watched as Brandson switched his gun from his left hand to the right one. With his free hand, he pulled a knife out of his pocket and put the blade so that its tip was pressed lightly against the woman's jugular.

Just like in her vision.

Her head began to swim. Flashes from her vision began overlaying reality and she could hardly breathe.

She wouldn't be fast enough. She knew that now. Even if she tripped and managed to come through the lights behind him with her knife intact, he'd still have time to kill that woman. All this foreknowledge didn't count for a hill of beans. It was all happening just like before, except that Balcher wasn't here.

She pulled away from her hiding place and walked out into the center of the garage where he could see her.

"I'm here," she said, holding her hands out to show she had no weapon, although the switchblade was still in her pocket. "Let her go."

Before he could answer, sounds of footsteps alerted both of them that someone was in the garage with them. Spooky turned in time to see Balcher point his gun at the Ice Man. Blood drained from her face and her heart nearly stopped.

Oh, no! Balcher! This can't be happening!

"Drop your weapon, Detective, or I'll slit this woman's throat," Brandson ordered.

Balcher eased up close to Spooky, and like he did two days ago on the casino's rooftop, he pushed her behind him. He threw a quick glance in her direction, his expression begging her to open up her mind to him.

Spooky couldn't deny him. Not now. She had to warn him! He didn't know what was going to happen! In her head, she imagined her mind melting and the iron just went away, leaving her totally open to the man she loved more than her own life. She felt Balcher's protectiveness close around her.

Trust me. I can do this. I know how because I saw it in your vision.

He shot you in my vision!

No, he didn't. Think about it. Please, sweetheart, you have to trust me!

Without waiting for her comprehension, Balcher turned back towards the Ice Man and then he tossed his gun about ten feet away. "You can let her go now," he told the Ice Man.

Spooky watched it all happen. It was just like before. Brandson ripped the blade across the woman's throat, and blood gushed as she fell to the ground convulsing. In the same moment, he pointed his gun at Balcher and pulled the trigger. She cried out, "*No...*"

"Stop!" Balcher screamed simultaneously.

Everything froze.

Balcher saw the bullet in mid-air, just inches from his chest, like it was frozen in time. If he wanted, he could have plucked it out of the air. The woman was on the ground ten feet away, her hand over her throat, the bright red blood spurting through her fingers, except that it was frozen as well. It was like a three-dimensional photograph, the droplets of blood hanging in the air just like the bullet.

He moved, but he was the only thing that was moving. No, that wasn't exactly true. Everything else was moving...in *Real Time*.

He was just moving faster. Faster than the speed of light.

Wow!

He reached into the air in front of him and touched the bullet.

Ouch!

Damned thing burned his fingers! He knocked it with the back of his hand and it moved up in the air about two feet. He hit it again and it went up further. He reached up and made sure it was pointed in a direction that wouldn't hurt anyone when Real Time started back up. That put the bullet in a trajectory pointed about twelve inches over his head.

Then he walked over to the Ice Man and just stood there watching him, fascinated. He could see minuscule movement, like a stop-action film played at super-slow speed. But since he didn't know how long he could sustain this trip outside of Real Time, he decided to get busy. He took the gun out of the Ice Man's right hand and, after putting the safety on, he laid it on the ground. Then he took the knife out of his other hand and put it beside the gun. Straightening up, he reached out and touched the cold son of a bitch. With his eyes closed, he concentrated hard on getting a vision. He knew that Spooky was better at this, but she was still back in Real Time.

Almost immediately, he began to get flashes, glimpses of the Ice Man's fantasy. The images had practically been dancing in the guy's head all day. He was so sure of his victory that he'd kept Spooky's identity a secret until he finalized the bidding.

Balcher winced. Some pretty scary people were now completely intrigued with the idea that there was a live human being who could teleport, and they all had copies of the video that the Ice Man had taken on the roof that day.

The video was grainy—those phone cameras were not the best at capturing something as important as this—but Balcher saw the Ice Man's reasoning for choosing that device. Casinos didn't allow cameras inside, but they couldn't refuse cell phones. Of course, most of the buyers disputed his evidence as shoddy, but they were all so enamored with the possibility of teleportation that they chose to stay in the bidding until the end. They were positively salivating to see Spooky for themselves.

Balcher's heart clenched. Spooky was right. There would always be people out there willing to use her for their own purposes. Cruel, inhuman people. Fortunately for Spooky and himself, they no longer resembled the people shown in that video, and it would be difficult, if not impossible, to locate them by the images that video contained.

He felt a resoluteness grow inside him. No one would ever find out that Spooky was the woman in that video. He would spend the rest of his life making sure of that.

Balcher was about to release his grip on the man when he caught another flash of a memory. He saw a Las Vegas bank in the guy's mind. And a safety deposit box number.

He jerked himself out of the trance, worried about connecting too strongly with the guy, and reached into the Ice Man's pocket to get his keys. He pulled the safety deposit box's key off of the key ring and then put the key ring back in his pocket.

Next was the hard part. He wasn't sure if he could do this. But, again, if he couldn't, he was sure that Spooky could.

He turned, went to the woman and knelt down by her side. With a persistent feeling of inadequacy still nagging at him, he reached out and laid his hands on her. He breathed in deep, and then with all the strength he could muster welling up from his heart, he reached into her mind and touched it, permeating the very core of the cells of her brain.

The connection was immediate.

He was suddenly somewhere else, floating through the images of her life and getting snatches of what made this woman the person she was.

He was there when her great, great, grandfather died, leaving her and her mother grief stricken. He was there when she got into medical school, and then again the first time she held a scalpel in surgery. He was there when her estranged husband beat her senseless and left her for dead. He was—

Balcher pulled himself out. The pain she had endured throughout the last four of her thirty-two years was horrific. Instead, he concentrated only on imagining that her throat wound was healed. Just that one thing. The image blurred and then began to glow.

He felt the lights coming—the very same lights he saw when he had tripped with Spooky. They seared through his brain and down his spine and out to his hands, and then directly into the woman's body. It was like an electrical jolt had passed between them.

He looked at her neck and the wound had seared shut. Cauterized.

It was all he knew to do and he prayed to God it was enough. He pulled his hands away from her, and then he got to his feet to approach the Ice Man one final time.

The guy's eyes were on his hands and there was a surprised expression on his face. Real Time had continued to move in minute increments while he was helping the woman, so the Ice Man knew from the disappearance of his weapons that something was happening that he could not control. He saw the comprehension on the guy's face. He saw the fear.

Good! He felt an immense satisfaction that the Ice Man had the realization that he was about to die. Balcher felt no pity. The Ice Man had slit that woman's throat with no remorse. He deserved none in return. But even with the anger simmering inside of him, Balcher felt a split-second of hesitation. Society gave him no right to be this man's executioner.

But, then again, if he only disarmed him, he would be signing Spooky's death warrant, as well as his own. Not to mention the millions of people that could possibly be affected if Spooky's gift got into the wrong hands. Teleportation would make the deadliest of terrorists. Nations would crumble, and empires would fall into the wrong hands.

With a deep breath, Balcher took the knife and slashed it across the Ice Man's jugular, cutting deep. The wound opened and Balcher could see the bone at the back of his neck gleaming through the blood.

His heart clenched with the pain of his lost innocence. From this point on, he would forever have blood on his hands. The same blood warriors over the centuries carried within their souls as they fought for the lives of their countries and their peoples.

The blood was not yet gushing out of the man's throat, but it would.

When he went back to Real Time.

With shaking hands, he cleaned his fingerprints off of the knife and then went to the woman. He pressed her fingers to the knife's handle and then placed the knife on the ground equidistant between her and the Ice Man. Then he picked up the gun and wiped his prints from it as well. He placed it in the holster inside the guy's jacket and that's when he found the other weapon. He pulled it out and looked at it. It was some kind of a dart gun.

Ah! He was planning to put Spooky to sleep. Well, that explained how he intended to deliver her to his auction. Balcher took that weapon and hid it underneath the tire-well of a nearby car. He would come back for it later.

He went back to stand in front of Spooky in the exact place he was standing before.

"Go!" he shouted, and Real Time resumed.

He heard the end of Spooky's scream and then her shocked astonishment when the bullet that had been fired directly at Balcher's heart hit the ceiling somewhere at the other side of the garage.

Balcher grabbed his head suddenly as excruciating pain ripped through his brain. For the briefest moment, he wondered if the bullet had still hit him, or worse yet, that he'd done something irrevocable to his mind by taking his trip outside of Real Time. Then the vice squeezing his brain lessened somewhat, leaving behind a terrible pounding, like he'd just gone ten rounds with a heavy-weight boxing champion. Before he could get a grip on what was happening to him, every muscle in his body cramped up, bringing him to his knees. Then, to top everything off, sudden hunger gnawed at him, twisting his stomach up in knots. He gritted his teeth, snarling in pain, even as his attention was caught by the sight of blood gushing from the Ice Man's throat.

It sprayed out, splattering onto the woman who was several feet away on the ground with her hand still on her throat. She flinched away from the red spray and scrambled to her feet, and then she suddenly froze, raising astonished eyes towards Balcher and Spooky. The astonishment turned into a strange sense of recognition.

"You healed—"

Don't say it out loud!

Balcher pushed the thought at her from his aching brain, knowing that she would hear him. By healing her, he had just touched her as intimately as Spooky had touched him when she took him through the lights. Even though his pain, he remembered that there were cameras in the parking garage, cameras that the police would know about and would surely be confiscating tapes from. Even though there was no audio, the cops would find someone to read her lips if the angle was right. God only knows how they were going to going to react to what they saw on that video tape. The action was not going to match the evidence on the scene.

The woman's eyes widened and Balcher saw the realization on her face that she'd just heard his thoughts in her head. Her mouth shut abruptly and then she turned to watch helplessly as the Ice Man convulsed on the cement floor.

Because she was a doctor, Balcher could feel her intense need to help the man at her feet, despite the fact that he had just tried to kill her. She restrained the impulse because she had Balcher's memories of the man and what he was planning to do to Balcher and Spooky. She didn't have to wait long. It was only moments until the Ice Man stopped jerking and a glassy look came over his eyes.

The next thing that happened had Balcher unconsciously forming a cross over his heart. The shadows that had been looming in the dark places around the garage slowly began to move in on the Ice Man's body. They surrounded him, seeping into his flesh until they seemed to disappear into the ground below him. The whole garage grew lighter and Balcher watched the transformation in wonder.

He glanced at Spooky and knew that she'd just seen the same thing. So did the woman. He scrambled to his feet, still groggy from pain, although it had lessened considerably.

They each stood there, immobilized, feeling as if their world had just shifted drastically in their presence, and that the reality they'd known their whole lives had forever changed beyond recognition. That is, until the sound of police sirens jerked them back into the real world.

Balcher listened as the sirens got louder, reverberating piercingly through the parking deck structure until four police cars screeched to a stop nearby, blue lights flashing.

"Get your hands up!" shouted the first patrolman to leave his car.

Balcher already had his badge out in his hand—he'd pulled it out as soon as he heard the sirens—but he raised his hands into the air as ordered. "I'm a detective with the LVPD," he shouted back in response. He was pretty much ignored as eight cops surrounded them, one going to the Ice Man to check his pulse, the rest of them keeping Balcher, Spooky and the woman in their gun sights.

"This one's dead," said the young officer who was bent over the Ice Man's body.

Balcher noticed that the boy, who could have been twenty at the most, hadn't felt for a pulse. He didn't blame him. Even as an experienced homicide cop, Balcher would have hesitated at searching for a pulse on that body. Besides, it was obvious from the amount of blood pooling around the victim's head that he was long gone from this world.

The boy, looking a little green at the sight of the gaping wound on the man's throat, went to stand up, but he stumbled and accidentally stepped into some of the blood. He quickly jumped back from the area only to leave bloody footprints on the floor's surface.

"Larry, you're such an idiot," yelled one of the other cops as he pulled the boy away and gave him a handkerchief to wipe the blood from his shoe.

Balcher didn't have time to be amused, though, because the other cops were starting to glance at him aggressively.

"Put your hands on this car over here and spread 'em," one of the patrolmen ordered him.

Balcher obeyed. He didn't want to give the trigger happy officers any excuse to shoot him, and then one of the other policemen motioned for the women to follow suit. They came to the car, put their hands on it and spread their legs out. They were all thoroughly searched, but the only one with a weapon on her person was Spooky. The cop's eyebrow lifted when he saw the switchblade. He placed it in an evidence bag and then placed that bag into a pouch that he threw over his shoulder.

Balcher said, "My service weapon's on the floor over there." He nodded his head towards the last place he saw his gun and one of the patrolmen went to look for it.

"Found it! It's standard issue, for sure. Looks just like mine." The officer who found his gun handed it over to one of the older cops. That cop walked over to where Balcher was still leaning over the car. "Let me see your badge."

The wallet with his badge in it was still in Balcher's hand. He tossed it to the officer and watched him flip it open. "Detective Michael Balcher," the officer read aloud, his expression quizzical.

One of the other guys looked up at the sound of Balcher's name. "Detective Balcher?" he said, coming around the front of the car. He looked Balcher over in astonishment. "I know this guy," he told the older officer. "At least, I think I do."

Balcher knew the officer by name. "Officer Hackett? I'm Zack's partner. We had a few beers together last month."

The guy nodded his head in skeptical remembrance. "You've lost a lot of weight since last week when I saw you at the station," he said, looking Balcher up and down. "And is that a wig?"

Balcher had the grace to look embarrassed. "A disguise," he explained. "Look, I can explain what's happened here. That's Spooky Knight," he said pointing to Spooky, "the private detective that works closely with Davenport on a regular basis.

"We were here looking for this guy," he straightened up from the car slowly and pointed at the Ice Man, "an industrial spy that she's been trying to catch for the last week. We tracked him down to this casino and I saw him at the blackjack tables. He spotted me and ran into the parking garage where he grabbed this woman," he said, indicating the woman with the long black hair.

"We confronted him and he tried to slit her throat with that knife. I'm not sure exactly what happened then. The next thing I knew, she grabbed for the guy's knife and swung around. Then she was on the ground and he was bleeding out of the neck. That's all I saw."

"That's what I saw, too," Spooky spoke up. "That's the knife he tried to use on the woman," she said pointing to the bloody knife lying on the ground near Brandson's body. "But, luckily, she managed to grab it and get him first. The guy's name is Nicholas Brandson. Winston Harrell, the casino manager, told me he was registered here. I was hoping to corner the guy here in the garage, and with Balcher's help, take him over to Radicom and find out who hired him to steal their new assembly process."

Officer Hackett looked at the black-haired woman. "And your name is?"

"Orenda Graycloud," the woman said. She had been remarkably quiet up to that point and Balcher saw her reluctance to tell the police anything at all, especially since his and Spooky's stories were not exactly the truth of what had happened. Actually, Balcher felt that she wasn't entirely sure what had happened. She was still in shock and not just from her near death experience.

"I really don't know what happened. I was headed for the elevator—I work in the casino as a money changer—when that man grabbed me around the neck. I screamed and then these two showed up. The man that grabbed me said he was going to slit my throat. I panicked and grabbed at the knife and tried to get away. The next thing I knew, I was on the ground. Blood was everywhere and I thought that I'd been cut, but then I saw that it was him and not me. He bled all over me," she said, her voice shaky as she told the truth as she saw it.

That's exactly right. Just tell them the truth as you know it. They can't trip you up that way.

Orenda almost looked at Balcher as his words came to her, but she managed to keep her eyes on the cop. "He almost killed me," she continued, blood leaving her face and turning her pale. Her voice was wispy with shock. "I can't believe any of this just happened."

At that moment, her knees buckled and one of the cops grabbed her around the waist to keep her from hitting the ground. He threw her arm over his shoulder and led her to his patrol car where he helped her into the back seat and gave her a bottle of water to drink.

Officer Hackett watched it all with a skeptical expression. Then he glanced at Balcher with a dead-pan look. "Sounds like everything's on the up and up. But we still gotta take you all in and get your statements."

"Of course," Balcher agreed, ignoring the young patrolman's sarcastic innuendo. He was still feeling nauseous from hunger and residual pain, but it didn't matter. He knew the drill. The cops were going to grill them unmercifully for a couple of hours until they had a grip on what had really happened in this garage. He knew what to expect because he was often the one doing the grilling. He looked pointedly at Spooky before saying aloud to the cop, "Let's go, Officer Hackett."

Both of you need to stay with the stories you just told them. Don't embellish. They won't believe what really happened so we all have to be extremely careful what we say. Agreed?

Balcher looked towards Orenda as she sat in the backseat of the patrol car. She nodded without looking at him. *Agreed.*

Agreed.

That second voice in his head was Spooky's. He turned towards her. She looked dazed that it was all finally over. Then he saw the gray in her mind come back. It looked like liquid metal filling in every crevice of her being. She was shielding herself from him again and the implications of the act made him frown.

"This way, Detective," Hackett said, leading Balcher to his car. He followed the officer, but watched as Spooky was taken to another vehicle. It was common procedure to separate witnesses so that they were not given the opportunity of comparing notes, although it was a little late for that now. Which is exactly why he spit out his story so fast a few minutes ago.

Balcher followed him and got into the back seat. He smelled food and his stomach clenched. "Got anything to eat?" he asked the officer. "I'm starving!"

Hackett gave him a strange look. "We'd just finished eating dinner when we got the call to come here. It's all gone."

Balcher growled and sat back in the seat. The hunger was an actual physical pain. He must have expended a huge amount of energy leaving Real Time and healing Orenda Graycloud. His body was nearly going into spasms as it fed on itself. He wasn't sure he could make it through the several hours the police would have him in interrogation. Well, he'd just have to, wouldn't he?

He held on until they got to the station and then, when they were about to go into the interrogation room, he made Hackett stop at the vending machines. He pulled out his wallet and pushed a bill into the slot and got one of his favorites; a Mars bar. Then he put another bill into the slot and got a pack of potato chips. He didn't stop there.

"What are you doing?" Hackett said as he watched Balcher grab the fifth candy bar out of the machine.

"I told you I was hungry," Balcher grumbled, placing the extra candy bars into his pocket and then opening one and practically devouring it whole in one bite.

He turned and ran straight into Zack. His partner was not exactly happy with him. Balcher had seen this expression on Zack's face many times before. Zack could act the fool better than anybody, but he was like a bulldog in the interrogation room. "You have a lot of 'splaining to do," Zack said. "And I can't wait to hear it."

Chapter Seventeen

Spooky sat anxiously on the uncomfortable rock-hard plastic bench in the corridor outside of the interrogation rooms. Detective Sanchez finished with her interrogation a half hour ago, thanks, she was sure, to Davenport's intervention. He'd come running into the interrogation room dressed in some mighty fine formal wear—he'd obviously been at some party or other—and whisked her out of the room for ten minutes to hear her side of things. The fact that he came to her first before he headed for the interrogation room where they were holding Balcher, said a lot about the man. He cared more about his psychic ace in the hole than he did about one of his own detectives.

Her case was also helped by the fact that the tape confiscated from the garage, even though it was filled with static, showed her nowhere near Brandson when he was cut. Of course, it didn't show Balcher close enough to do the deed, either.

They had watched her expression as she watched the tape playing, obviously hoping to provoke her into explaining the visual discrepancies displayed on the film. She sat there, silent, as she watched the distorted, static-filled, black and white images of Brandson cutting the Graycloud woman and throwing her to the ground. Then she watched him taking a shot at Balcher, which was where the tape went wacko. All of a sudden, the knife was on the ground and Brandson was grabbing his own throat and Balcher fell to his knees like he'd been shot. Of course, everyone knew that Balcher had not been shot because there was no injury to be found on him anywhere.

The detectives had been flabbergasted at the visual evidence and Spooky had felt every eye in the room concentrated intensely on her reaction to the tape. She did her best to look confused. It wasn't hard because she was confused. She didn't know how Balcher did it, so in that regard, she was every bit as flabbergasted as the rest of the people in the room.

Davenport, with his fore-knowledge of Spooky's psychic abilities, narrowed his eyes at her strangely throughout the whole interview. If she could have read his mind, she would have bet he was wondering if she had the power of telekinesis and had somehow used her ability to kill Brandson from a distance. But even if he felt the need to postulate that idea aloud, he couldn't have proved his theory.

Davenport was a smart man. He kept his mouth shut and the interview was over.

Spooky sat on that hard bench waiting for Balcher, not in the least worried about being arrested. She knew that she was in the clear, as were Balcher and the woman. With that tape in evidence, no jury would ever convict either one of them for anything.

She was, however, worried about the rumors that were sure to start up. People were going to start talking and when that happened, she was sure they were going to come up with some mighty strange conclusions. She didn't need or want the controversy. Not to mention that if any of Brandson's friends came investigating, they would hone in on her and Balcher like a duck on a June bug.

She wished she could leave the police station and go home, but she couldn't. She had to be here to see how it all came out. Plus the fact that she was finding it difficult to pull herself away from the mental conversation going on between Balcher and Orenda Graycloud. At least, Balcher's side of it. She couldn't hear the woman.

He sounded so gentle with Orenda, so protective. They were in separate rooms being interrogated separately, but Balcher was somehow managing to keep his mind on both conversations. He couldn't possibly be hearing the detective's side of her conversation, so

Spooky imagined that Orenda was telling Balcher what question they asked and then repeating his answer to them.

That he could stay on top of both conversations at the same time was no surprise to Spooky. Balcher was truly intelligent and in the last few days, he had amazed her in so many ways.

How many men could have dealt so quickly with what she'd just put him through? How many would have accepted the paranormal so easily, even to the point of finding out they were suddenly psychic, too? Balcher acted like his abilities were just new toys he'd inherited, almost like they were something to play with and be entertained by.

Not that he was not a careless man, but she wondered if he considered the ramifications of what he did when he healed Orenda.

She also wondered if he had given any thought to the depth of betrayal she would feel because of what he did with Orenda. Not necessarily the healing part, but the deep connection he'd had to forge with the woman to bring about the healing. Because now he was as intimately connected with Orenda Graycloud as he was with her. Touching minds and merging emotions, that was much more intimate than sex.

He'd had no choice but to heal the woman, Spooky knew that, but she was past being logical at the moment. All she knew was that the future that she saw and had been so desperately counting on with Balcher was suddenly up in the air.

And Orenda Graycloud was such a beautiful woman.

Balcher might not realize it, but he has a choice before him now. There are two women connected intimately with him and Spooky was not at all sure that he would choose her.

Spooky felt tears well up in her eyes and she blinked them away in irritation. Crying never has and never would help any problem that has ever been set before her. It didn't help her mother, that was for sure. No, she had to hold it together...be strong...for Balcher and for herself, and for this new woman. Because, like it or not, she was ultimately responsible for what happened to Orenda Graycloud.

She sat up straight on the bench. She would let Balcher decide what to do about his own future and she would make damned sure that he would not be getting any pressure from her. He didn't owe her a thing. She saved his life and he's saved hers. They were even.

She would do fine without him.

Sure she would.

A half hour later, Balcher came out of his interrogation and saw Spooky waiting in the outside corridor. He was almost surprised to find her there. Even without being able to read her psychically, he felt sure that she was fairly jumping with the need to disappear into a safe place where she could gather her wits about her.

He sat down beside her. "They're still questioning Orenda," he said, watching as Zack headed for the squad room to write up his report. His partner hadn't been in the best of moods when he got here and he was furious with Balcher at this point because too many things were not adding up.

The two tapes from the casino's parking garage cameras were of very little use to the police because the action caught on the videos did not match the evidence at the scene. Zack was with the video expert when he first checked out the tapes and it was scientifically determined that there was no discernible editing or tampering on either of those tapes. Still, neither man could figure out why Brandson had a knife one second and the next it was on the floor several feet away without ever coming near his neck which had somehow just been slashed.

Then there was the issue of the drastic changes in both Spooky's and his own appearances. That was not going down well with anybody. Especially when there was no 'doctor' in Atlanta they could refer the investigators to. The general consensus in the station was that something really strange was going down in their midst, but no one was willing to utter any conjecture as to what that strangeness could mean.

"Yes, I know. I've been hearing your side of your conversation with her." Spooky said, avoiding his eyes.

Balcher's mind jumped from his worries about the police to Spooky and his eyes narrowed at her indifferent tone. "I couldn't leave her to those wolves in there. She's still reeling from what happened to her," he explained.

Spooky shrugged and then, still avoiding his gaze, she fiddled with a hang nail as if nothing he said was of any importance to her.

Balcher was confused at her behavior, but something about her exacts words confused him more. "How come you could hear what I was thinking, but not hear her?"

"I didn't connect with her the way you did," she said. "I can't read her mind."

Ah, so that was it! He was finally getting the picture and he was surprised that he hadn't considered this earlier. He should have. He should have known what it would mean to Spooky for him to connect so deeply with another woman. Connecting with Orenda was an intimate act. Not cheating, exactly, but in some ways, it was worse than cheating.

Spooky had a right to feel betrayed by him. In her view—even though she had to know that it couldn't have been helped—this just as bad as if he'd had an affair.

He understood Spooky's fears perfectly because he *had* connected with Orenda. And, in doing so, he'd forged a closeness with her. He felt protective of her. He even loved her like an old friend.

But—and he had better come up with a way to prove this to Spooky—he didn't want Orenda. He felt no sexual interest in her whatsoever. And even though these feelings he had for Spooky were new, he knew that there was no way that he could ever love Orenda or any other woman as deeply as he loved Spooky.

He probed at Spooky's mind, but it was still gray to him. "How could you hear my thoughts when I can't get through to you?" he asked.

She shrugged. "I've learned a new trick. It allows me to shield my mind and be able to use my gifts at the same time."

"Why do you need to shield your mind from me, Spooky?" he asked, trying to be gentle with her. She looked so fragile, as if she could splinter apart at any moment.

She shrugged her shoulders again. "The crisis is over now. We've got to make a start on separating ourselves. We can't spend the rest of our lives attached at the hips."

Her words sent a shiver of fear through him. She was attempting to sever him from her life and he couldn't let her do that.

He said, "Not attached at the hips, no. But we will spend the rest of our lives attached at the heart." He reached out to turn her face to his because without the ability to read her mind, he needed to see her eyes.

"How can you be so sure of that," Spooky asked, her eyes darkening to a deep gray-blue. "Orenda Graycloud is a beautiful woman. What if she needs you?"

"Then I'll be there for her, like I would for any old friend," he assured her. "But you are the only woman I want to spend the rest of my life with. I think, somewhere deep down in my soul, that I knew that even before we tripped together. I've been fascinated with you since the day I met you; I was just too stubborn to give into the fascination. It's that connection you told me about. It's always been there. I love you, Spooky," he said, his heart in his eyes.

Tears welled up and fell from her eyes. "You don't know that. You could feel differently six months down the road. We've—"

He interrupted her with a hint of aggravation in his voice. "I know how I feel. And you'd know it, too, if you'd only let your mind go free and hold onto my hand. You could see for yourself exactly how I feel about you."

Just at that moment, Orenda came out of the third interrogation room. She nodded to them in passing and Spooky could see that she was thinking something to Balcher. She couldn't hear what the woman thought, but she could feel Balcher's protective instincts well up in response. Still, he didn't answer her telepathically which was certainly interesting. Hiding his response from her was a bad omen.

"Orenda, wait up," Balcher said, standing up. "We can ride together to the casino to get our cars. No point in tying two patrol cars up." He reached down and grabbed Spooky's hand and dragged her along behind him as he hurried to catch up with the woman.

Spooky resisted, trying to break his hold, but it was like being pulled behind a bull. She didn't want to ride to the casino with Balcher and the woman. She absolutely didn't want to be witness to any more tenderness being shared between the two of them.

Balcher tossed a frustrated glance backwards at Spooky and ordered, "You're coming with us. We're going to get this settled once and for all."

Spooky had never seen that look on Balcher's face before in all the years she'd known him. He was angry. With a pout that she could not keep off of her face, she gave up fighting him and got into the patrol car with them. Balcher sat in front with the patrolman and Orenda sat in the back seat with her. Spooky nodded politely to the woman as they rode to the casino in silence.

She hated herself for feeling this jealousy. She also felt guilty because none of this was Orenda's fault, but it didn't help the resentment she felt. She wanted it to go away. She wanted to be able to talk to Orenda and smile and be nice, but all she could think about was that Balcher was going to realize that Orenda was a better choice and that he'd be a fool to give up a normal woman like Orenda for a misfit like her.

Spooky was glad when the patrolman dropped them off at the entrance to the casino parking deck. Sitting in the back seat, so closely confined with the other woman, was bringing goose bumps to her arms and neck. The woman was sending out powerful vibes, but Spooky was having trouble reading them.

Spooky ran her hands up and down her arms as she stood fidgeting there under the parking lot lamppost. The night was barely cool, but the goose bumps would not go away. She looked at Orenda and saw that she was almost shivering.

"You don't have to go in there if you don't want to," Balcher said to Orenda, knowing that the parking garage had to hold fearsome memories for her. "I can go get your car and pull it out here for you."

Spooky watched as the woman straightened her spine, pulling herself together. She shook her head. "I can do it."

Balcher looked pointedly at Spooky and then led Orenda to a nearby bench. "I'm sure you can. But first, let's sit here a minute." He sat down beside Orenda and then motioned for Spooky to take a seat on his other side. "We'd like to talk to you about what's happened to you."

Orenda looked at him and then at Spooky. With a deep sigh, she said, "I pretty much have the picture. I saw...um...in my head...what the two of you have been going through for the last couple of days."

Spooky blushed. If Orenda saw everything, then she also saw them making love. Her embarrassment at the situation just doubled. She rushed into an explanation. "This...*thing*...that Balcher shared with you, saved your life. If he hadn't connected with you at the level he did, you would have died."

"I realize that," Orenda said. "Will I be changed in the same way he was?"

"I don't know," Spooky answered, surprised at the woman's level of understanding. She shouldn't be surprised; she knew how the connection worked first hand. One minute the person beside you is a stranger, the next, they practically knew you inside, out.

Orenda had a calmness about her that was eerie, but Spooky sensed a great sadness underneath the composure. "It depends on your own personal brain chemistry, how you were wired to begin with, so to speak. We believe that people with some kind of paranormal background are affected at a deeper level. Do you have anyone in your family that you would have called psychic?"

Orenda smiled and the smile altered her sad face significantly. She was an astonishingly beautiful woman. "My great-great-grandfather belonged to the False Face Society of the Cayuga tribe of the Haudenosaunee people. You may know them as Iroquois. The False Face Society was sort of what you'd call medicine men. My grandfather had a powerful healing gift. That's why I went into medicine, to honor him."

"I've never heard of the False Face Society," Spooky said, interested despite herself.

"They are called that because of the magical masks they wear, masks that give them their power," Orenda explained.

"Oh," Spooky said, although she really didn't comprehend it all. In all her paranormal research, Indian mythology was the most mysterious to her. "Then that may have some bearing on how you have been changed. Of course, there's no guarantee that you will be any different at all. Um...besides the ability to speak telepathically with Balcher, that is."

"He loves you, you know?" Orenda said, changing the subject and sending a level look at Spooky. "As a woman, I can imagine what you're feeling, right now. But you don't have to worry. There's a great big 'I'm taken' sign hanging inside his head."

Spooky's eyes grew big. "Was that just a guess, or did you get something, a flash, from sitting here on this bench with me."

"It was an educated guess. All I see when I look at you is this aura of grayness. It's like you've blocked the light from touching you," Orenda said as sadness once more settled onto her face.

Spooky looked away, but she could feel Balcher's gaze on her. "I... can't take my shields down yet. I need time to think all of this through, first."

So much had happened in one day, and it was all happening too fast for Spooky to get a handle on it. First, she and Balcher defeated the Ice Man and Balcher had somehow pulled it off with an ability that Spooky had no clue about. The interrogations at the police station were both exhausting and frightening given their potential for eventual exposure. On top of that, Spooky was now dealing with a most horrific bout of jealousy, jumbling her emotions into a tight ball.

And she was responsible for it all because she was somehow passing along something that was infecting people with the psychic gene or at least activating those who were already psychically wired.

She couldn't think! There was so much to consider. She was jumpy to the point that she could barely focus. Still, she owed this woman something because, whether she liked it or not, she was now forever connected with her, too.

She glanced back towards Orenda. "My name is Spooky Knight and my cell phone number is in the phone book. I want you to call me anytime you have questions or need my help in any way." Her voice caught for a moment as her throat tightened, constricting her air flow. Her heart was beating fast and Spooky realized that she was probably suffering from the beginnings of an anxiety attack. If so, it was the first one ever. "But right now, I really need to get home. I have to...to think...and I need to eat."

That said, she jumped up and ran into the parking garage. She dived into the elevator at the ground floor and hit the button for the fourth level before Balcher could catch up with her.

She was shaking. She'd been alone for so many years and even though the last two days have been frightening, they'd also been the best days of her life. Balcher meant everything to her. She didn't know how she could go back to the way it was before. She bent over, trying to breathe normally, frustrated that her anxiety in losing Balcher was taking on this physical form. She really shouldn't have been surprised, so much of what she had felt over the years manifested itself physically with her.

Balcher must realize by now that he had the whole world to choose from, that he'd be a fool to stay with her. No man would choose her on purpose; she was a pitiful misfit and a lightening rod for trouble! Even though Brandson was dead, how many others would come looking for her? It was never going to end. Balcher deserved better than to be stuck with her!

The elevator stopped and the door opened and Spooky ran for her car. She hadn't locked it, and her keys were still on the driver's seat where she'd left them. She cranked up and was about to pull out of the parking space when she had to slam on her brakes.

Balcher was standing behind her car with his arms crossed over his chest and he had a fiercely determined expression on his face as he met her gaze in the rear view mirror.

I'm not letting you go anywhere without me. You'll have to run over me to get out of here.

She hit the steering wheel in frustration. She was almost light-headed from lack of oxygen from her constricted throat and didn't know what to do. If she lowered her shields, he would know what she was thinking. But without that, he wouldn't trust anything she said.

Get out of the car, Spooky. Come around and give me your keys. I'll drive you home.

She didn't have a choice because she couldn't sit in her car all night. And knowing Balcher, he would stand there until she did as he asked. She yanked her keys out of the ignition and then threw open her car door and got out.

"You have no right to force me, Balcher. I don't want to be near you right now," she muttered as she rounded the back fender of her car.

"I don't have to *see* what you're thinking to *know* what you're thinking, Spooky. You've forgotten how well I know you," he said as she closed in on him. He held out his hand out for her keys.

She tossed them at him. "If you really knew me, you'd know that I need to be alone right now."

He smirked. "Alone to hide? Like you've always done when it comes to opening up and letting anyone into your life?"

"If so, that's my business," she muttered, frustrated that he did, indeed, know her so well.

"Come here," he said grabbing her and pulling her against his chest.

Spooky fought the contact for a moment and then relaxed when she felt the anxiety lessening and her ability to breathe come back. His touch alone was enough to calm her.

"So, you're telling me that you have no interest in seeing the rest of this Ice Man business finished?" he whispered into her ear, knowing that she wouldn't be able to resist that particular carrot. Sure enough, her interest was perked.

"What do you mean?" she asked, pushing out of his embrace and crossing her arms defensively in front of her chest.

"Get in the car, and I'll tell you what I saw when I touched him outside of Real Time," Balcher said. He knew he had her now. If anything, Spooky was intensely curious.

She frowned, but got into the drivers side and sat behind the wheel as ordered.

Balcher went to the passenger side and got in. He closed the door and then handed her the car keys. "Drive around until you see Renda. She's worried about you and I want to let her know that you're okay. Plus, we need to set up a time next week to talk to her about a couple of things. We can't just leave her hanging."

"Renda?" Spooky asked, resisting the rest of the jealous quip she wanted to throw at him as she cranked the car and pulled out of the parking space.

"Her nickname," Balcher muttered patiently as Spooky drove around the fourth level of the garage until she saw Orenda waiting beside her car.

Spooky pulled up beside the woman and rolled down her window. "I'm sorry for running out on you. It's just been a bad day all around." Her tone was not the most gracious, but she saw understanding on Orenda...*Renda's* face.

Balcher leaned across Spooky's chest to look out of the driver's side window. "Come see me at the station next Monday. I'll bring you to Spooky's house and we'll talk all of this out. We can help you with Alexander, Renda. You're not alone in this any longer."

Renda flinched when he mentioned Alexander and Spooky's curiosity notched up a bit higher. Apparently, there was still a great deal about this situation that she was not aware of.

Renda nodded and then hurriedly got into her car. The bad vibes from the place were obviously getting to her.

Spooky backed up so that Renda could pull out and then she followed her out of the parking deck. "What was that all about?" she asked Balcher as she memorized the woman's license plate. Old habits died hard.

"You can't read my mind and figure it out?" he asked with a trace of sarcasm.

"No," she frowned, puzzled. "Why can't I?" she wondered aloud, as she headed her car for the nearest Taco Bell. As usual, she was hungry and comfort food was just the thing for what ailed her at the moment.

"Because I've figured out your trick," Balcher said, obviously pleased with himself. "Every time I've tried to see what you're thinking, all I see is this metallic dark-gray substance. So, knowing how you think, I tried imagining what I'd do if I were you. Then it came to me. You're imagining your brain is made of steel. I tried it and tested it by tossing a few thoughts at you. You didn't even flinch. So I know that it works."

"So what? I never said you weren't smart," she said, her stomach growling as she spied the Taco Bell sign in the distance. Funny how even in the most depressing times, thoughts of food could perk her right up.

"Why don't you pull into that Taco Bell up there?" Balcher asked, pointing towards the sign. "I'm starving."

Spooky smiled. Even when he couldn't read her mind, he knew what she was thinking. "What do you want," she asked, rolling her window down as she pulled into the parking lot and up to the drive-thru menu. Food was serious business. Their argument could continue later.

"Just double your order," he said, smiling back at her.

With several bags of food—half of which wouldn't make it back to her house, she was sure—they left the Taco Bell and headed for home.

Spooky felt the usual cloak of security come over her as she pulled into her driveway. The only thing that bothered her was having to let Balcher into the house with her. As she usually did when she brought food home with her, she sat in her favorite spot on the couch in her living room and spread the remainder of the food out on her coffee table. Then she pulled her legs beneath her and grabbed the TV remote. Just because he was here, it didn't mean she had to listen to him.

Balcher joined her on the sofa, amused at her antics. If she thought she could freeze him out, she had another think coming.

Still, he could wait until she was no longer hungry. He'd learned by experience not to get between Spooky and her food!

When the food was all gone, Balcher gathered up all the wrappers and stuffed them in the bag they came in. Then he looked pointedly at Spooky and saw the wall of irritation she had waiting for him. "Well, what do you want to talk about first? Us or the Ice Man business?"

"Real Time," she said, reluctantly interested. Even in her distress, her mind had been consistently coming back to that subject. "How'd you do it and what was it like?" she asked, practically spitting the words out.

Balcher smiled. He had actually already figured that would be her first choice of topics. "Real Time is like we are now. It's the natural pace of the universe. But in that parking garage, I went outside of Real Time. I was in some kind of accelerated mode, moving faster than light."

Spooky's expression change from irritation to astonishment.

Balcher smiled. "Actually, to explain better, I need to go back to the beginning...the night you had your vision. I was asleep when you had it—"

"So was I," she interrupted him. "I dreamed the whole thing, and then woke up in a cold sweat right as Brandson shot you."

"He shot *at* me," Balcher corrected her. "You saw the bullet as it froze in mid-air. Admit it," he said, raising an eyebrow at her.

She frowned. "Yes, that's what I saw. But I knew that you were going to be killed because the bullet was headed right for your chest. You couldn't have moved fast enough to get out of the way."

Balcher raised a brow. "Well, that's not exactly true, as you well know. But to get back to my story, I woke up with you gone and then the hotel staff was feeding me this ridiculous story about me being a dope addict," he said, and watched as Spooky tried to choke a grin at her part in that fiasco.

She couldn't hold the amusement in any longer and she burst out laughing. "I was particularly proud of coming up with that. I know how persuasive you are, so I needed a convincing story."

"Yeah, well, you found one," he said, frowning at the memory. "Anyway, there I was, pacing around that danged room, totally pissed off, and then I sat down in the chair by the window and boom!

Flashes of your vision hit me in the head."

"You saw my vision through touching that chair?" she said. Why didn't she remember that he was clairvoyant? She should have remembered that!

He nodded. "I knew what you were going to do and I knew I had to stop you. So, I found a pay phone, called Zack, and had him arrange a flight home for me. When I got here, he picked me up at the airport and then dropped me off at the casino to get my car. That's when I saw the Ice Man. I knew if I followed him, I'd find you."

"And you did," she said with a heavy sigh.

"And I did. I knew that you'd left me in Atlanta to protect me. But what you didn't understand—I guess, because you really weren't meant to understand—was that time really had stopped in your vision. So, I let everything happen just as we both saw it, and then when he pointed his gun at me and pulled the trigger, I yelled 'stop.'"

"That's it? You just said 'stop?'" she asked.

He smiled. "Yeah. I knew from your experience with tripping that simplicity is the key to everything," he said.

"That's not what I meant. I would have thought that you—as a cop, I mean—would have yelled 'freeze!'" she said with a smirk.

"Funny," he growled. "But that didn't occur to me. Anyway, even the word 'stop' was not appropriate. Because time didn't stop for me, it just stopped around me. I pushed the bullet out of harm's way and then went to the Ice Man—"

"His name's Nicholas Brandson," she interrupted him.

"Brandson, then. So I went to Brandson and after taking his weapons away from him, I touched him to get a vision. I was hoping I could see if he'd passed along any information about you to anyone."

"And did you?"

"Yes. He had tapes made of us taking a header off of that roof and then disappearing into thin air. He gave them out to several people, although I didn't push hard enough to see if I could find out who they were. Like you, I was afraid to connect with him too deeply. I didn't want to let any of his coldness infect me." He shivered.

"Anyway, I know the tape he had was not a very good one and that they weren't completely convinced that we were the real thing."

Spooky's heart started racing again. This was her worst nightmare. "Oh, God! They'll find us!"

Balcher held a hand up. "Don't panic. You and I don't look the same anymore, remember? And the quality of the video from that cell phone was grainy, so unless they know exactly where to look for us, that tape isn't going to be any help at all."

"But he probably told them my name!" she said, miserably.

He shook his head. "He was a smart man, so he wouldn't do that. You can trust me on that, sweetheart. For one thing, I saw in his head that he withheld all the pertinent facts about you. But even if I hadn't seen that, it would only make sense that he wouldn't have told them who you were. If he'd given anyone your name and location, they could have found you without his help and he would have lost out on his big payday."

"That's all you saw?" she asked.

"That and a safety deposit box number at a bank here in Vegas. I'm going to check it out tomorrow."

"You're positive that you didn't go too deep?"

"Into his mind, you mean?" He shook his head. "No. I stayed as shallow as I could and be able to get the information we needed."

"But you did go deep with Renda, didn't you?" she asked.

He nodded. "I had to. I didn't know how else to help her. I put everything I had into it, concentrating on her wound healing, and I saw the lights again. They went through me and into her."

"You saw her life, felt her pain. You know her mind intimately," she said.

He narrowed his eyes. "Yes, I saw her life and her pain. And she saw ours. You and I are wrapped so tightly together that she couldn't have separated us if she tried."

"You care about her." It was a statement, not a question.

"Yes, I do. Like a sister or a good friend. But not as a lover." He reached out and touched her arm, letting the back of his fingers trail down her sensitive skin.

Spooky shivered at the touch. "You could be her lover, if you wanted to. Or any other woman's lover. You're not bound to me."

His fingers stopped. He reached out with both hands and gripped her arms, lifting her into his lap where he held her snuggly against him. "Actually, I am bound to you. I'm bound in a way that neither you nor I will ever be able to sever," he whispered into her ear.

She trembled. Even with her defenses up, she felt the connection with Balcher's flesh. "You can't know that. There could be someone out there that you are meant to be with, but you just don't know it yet."

He growled, "I know who I'm meant to be with, Spooky. So do you. Can you imagine being with anybody but me?"

The thought startled her. She could not imagine anyone but him. Not even Davenport interested her any longer. The crush she had on Davenport over the last few years did not belong in the same stratosphere as her feelings for Balcher. "No, but—"

He kissed her. Lightly. Then with his mouth just inches from hers, he whispered, "How you felt, just now when I asked you that question, is how I feel when you tell me that I'll find someone else. It's just not possible for me to love anyone else the way I love you. Not Renda, and not any other woman, either. No one will even come close to how much I love you."

He kissed her again and he felt her began to melt. The grayness was going away. His mouth moved from her lips to her ear, "I want you. I'll always want you, nobody else." He lifted her again, this time to straddle her over his lap, one leg on either side of his thighs. He pulled her hips in close so that she could feel how much he wanted her.

The grayness went completely away and he felt the connection immediately. They were merging emotionally, if not physically at the moment. "What we have together is not possible with another woman, sweetheart, no matter how many women I connect with in the future. None of them will share this with me, only you."

Spooky felt the truth of what he was saying. Since this was her first time actually connecting with him since he healed Renda, she was finally able to see what happened between them.

Balcher was right. The connection he shared with Orenda was that of an old friend. There was no sexual chemistry, at all.

She felt a tremendous relief, but it was soon followed by a torrent of desire. Desire that was intermingled with the love she felt for him and from him. He did love her; she felt it coming at her in waves and it was so much more powerful that any strong feelings that he kept in his heart for everyone else. Balcher had a powerful capacity for love and for loyalty and he was giving of them freely to her.

With tears in her eyes, Spooky wrapped her arms around him and held him close to her heart. "I love you, Michael."

He chuckled, and the sound made his chest rumble. "You've never called me Michael before...*Sarah*."

She pulled away to look him in the eyes. "I've never been able to say 'I love you' before, either. Not to anybody, even my mother. Maybe because she never said it to me."

"She loved you, sweetheart. I remember that from your memories."

"I know she did. She just never said it." Spooky looked down at the button on his shirt, almost afraid of the compassion she would see in Balcher's eyes. Then she realized that she didn't need to ever fear anything from him again. She could share her heart and all the pain that went with it. She looked back up at him. "I think she felt guilty over what she did to me. That, and the drugs, made her into someone that couldn't deal with her feelings, even those for her own child."

Balcher said, "Our children will know we love them, Sarah."

Spooky was startled. "Are you sure you want children with me? I mean, we have no idea what kind of gifts they'll have. There's no telling what we'll be releasing onto the world," she said.

"If there are children, then we'll love them and we'll teach them how to handle their gifts."

Spooky said, "It's a hard life...being different. Maybe we should wait a while before we decide to become parents."

Balcher shrugged. "We'll discuss it again after you marry me."

Spooky couldn't help it. A big grin lit up her face and she leaned in and kissed him for all she was worth. Knowing she was loved was the best thing, of course, but marriage implied trust in that love. It took a great deal of faith to make such a commitment and Balcher just gave that gift of faith to her.

She ended the kiss to breathe, and then she giggled. "Your friends at the police department are never going to let you live this down! Married to the 'Spookster'. Huh!"

Balcher grinned. "I don't care what they think. Besides, I'm interviewing for another job next week."

"Oh, yeah? Where?" Spooky asked, surprised.

"At the Spooky Knight Detective Agency," he answered with a wink. "I've got an 'in' with the boss there."

She laughed aloud. "Oh, you do, do you? I hear that lady's crazy! She thinks she's psychic or something!"

"Oh, she's crazy, all right. She's going to marry me."

"She's crazy like a fox," Spooky said, moving in for another kiss. The kiss turned into something much more explosive and it was only minutes before the two of them were naked and in her bed.

Spooky was on her back with Balcher riding firmly between her thighs, both of them still experiencing the same beautifully awesome sensations from both sides.

Lightning.
Thunder.
Pounding.
Throbbing.
Release.
Blessed release...

Long minutes later, Spooky snuggled sleepily against Balcher's chest in the aftermath of lovemaking. "I hope it's always this way between us," she said.

"It will be," he said with certainty. "It's not like our fading memories. Those *should* fade into the background. But this is the way lovemaking should be, the way it was probably meant to be from the beginning for everyone."

She raised her head to look at him. "Are you saying that we...you and I...are the way people are supposed to be, but that something happened and most of the population lost their ability to...uh...be like us?"

He shrugged. "Maybe...I don't know. I just know that it feels right, what we have. And that I wouldn't trade it for all the normalcy in the world."

Spooky laid her head back on his chest. "So, you're saying that maybe it's not a bad thing that I've...*changed*...you, and maybe some other people, too?"

"You're still worried about that, aren't you?" he asked.

She replied, "Yes. Not so much about you, and maybe even Renda, or even Jenny from the hair salon, but that lady kidnapper from the police station, last week, disturbs me."

"That will be our first assignment at the Spooky Knight Detective Agency. We'll look up some of your old cases where you've come into close personal contact with the clients and check them all out. If we find anything disturbing, we deal with it then. Okay?"

"Okay."

"We'll start with the kidnapper. She's still in lock-up as far as I know. We'll go to the station tomorrow morning. I'll turn in my badge—I'm actually looking forward to that part—and then we'll pay the woman a quick visit."

She said, "And then, after her, we check out all the rest of them?"

"No, after I turn in my badge and we check out the kidnapper, we go find Elvis and tie the knot."

"Elvis?"

"Or any other wedding chapel in Vegas. I don't care which one, just as long as you are permanently and legally tied to me by the end of the day, tomorrow," Balcher said, kissing her soundly. He knew that Spooky didn't expect or want a big wedding, and that even the thought of it was outlandish to her. That was fine by him. This way, he'd have her securely wrapped up and in the shortest time possible.

"You are such a romantic," she groaned. "So, Elvis is gonna marry us, huh?"

"Well, actually, his name is Ricardo. He's a buddy from way back. But he does a wonderful Elvis impersonation. And he makes a credible living out of it. So, what do you say?"

"Elvis, here we come!"

Chapter Eighteen

Zack tossed the birdseed like a pro. "I still can't believe you just did this, buddy," he said to Balcher as he followed the two of them from the wedding chapel. Elvis/Ricardo was singing *Love Me Tender* in the background and there was a white limo with 'Just Married' signs and streamers tied from every conceivable place parked right out front.

"Believe it, my friend. I've found the woman of my dreams," Balcher said, taking Spooky's hand and helping her into the limo. When they were both in, they stuck their heads out of the sun roof.

"Catch, Zack," Spooky yelled, throwing her bouquet in his direction as the limo pulled away. It hit him square in the chest and he grabbed at it. When he realized what he'd done, he tossed the offending flower spray to the ground and looked around to make sure nobody saw him catch it.

"That was not funny!" he called after the limo, shaking his fist in the air.

Giggling, Spooky ducked back through the sun roof and fell onto the backseat of the posh limo, pulling Balcher with her. "He is such a hoot!" she laughed.

"Can you believe he got all of this ready in two hours?" Balcher said, kissing his new bride before looking her up and down in admiration of her fancy white satin wedding gown.

"You can thank Francesca—or is it Frank?—for the dress," Spooky said, still giggling. "She...uh, he...seems quite taken with Zack."

Balcher snorted. "I know. Isn't it hilarious? Zack runs from her every time we see her, but she was the first person he thought of when we told him we were getting married today."

"So, Zack doesn't go that way?"

"Nope. Why do you think he made *you* call her?"

She laughed. "It has been kind of fun, hasn't it. I mean, if I'd have had to worry about a big wedding, I wouldn't have made it. But this was actually fun."

"Even the part where we saw the kidnapping bimbo this morning?" he asked, hesitating to bring up a touchy subject, but wanting to get it out in the air and over with.

"Even with that," she said, her smile disappearing as she considered the strange morning they'd had. The woman had been changed, but it was not something that Spooky had anticipated. She had apparently been given the ability to see the shadows. It was a horrifying gift for someone who had done so much evil in her life. She could probably see the light—or 'path' as Spooky and Balcher called it—if she'd tried, but she was too afraid of the shadows to give anything else a chance.

They'd watched her silently from a distance as she moved around her cell trying to escape them this morning. Her terror was so vivid... so palpable...that neither Spooky nor Balcher needed to get any closer to check her out. And they saw the shadows, too, as they lurked around the woman.

"What do you think would happen if they managed to get into her?" she asked Balcher.

"I don't think they can. At least, not until she's dead like the Ice Man. I think they hover around people who have given into evil and just wait for their demise. That's why it was so dark in the parking garage yesterday evening. They followed Brandson there."

"Actually, they gathered there waiting for him," she said, and then another thought occurred to her. "Do you think that woman might still have a chance? That maybe she can turn her life around and escape them?"

"Maybe. She has to want to change, though. I don't see that happening. She's going to jail for kidnapping. Those places have got to be filled with shadows," he said.

She asked, "Can we help her?"

Balcher sighed. "Sweetheart, it would be wonderful if we could, but I don't think it's possible. You've been like this your whole life. How often have you seen the shadows?"

"They've always been there, but rarely tied to a particular person like they were with that woman and with the Ice Man."

Balcher said, "I think that when a human being makes a conscious decision to do evil, they invite them in. It's not something that just happens to people because they've made a mistake or fell into trouble. It can't be easy to get rid of them, sweetheart, so you can't let yourself dwell on the lost causes of the world. There are going to be plenty of people we can help. Concentrate on those people and leave the rest to their fate."

"People like Renda?" Spooky asked. She was no longer jealous of Renda, but she was worried about her. And since Spooky didn't have her shields up, Balcher knew she was okay with the subject.

"Yeah, people exactly like Renda. You know, I don't think she was actually surprised by all of this. Did you get a sense of that?" he asked as he took her hand, the one with the wedding band branding her as his, into his own. He couldn't sit near Spooky without feeling the compulsion to touch her. And if she didn't have such an outdated sense of propriety, he would have pulled her onto his lap by now.

She felt his longing, but tried to ignore it for now. "What do you mean?"

Balcher smiled. He liked it that she knew that he wanted her even if she was too embarrassed to give into her inclinations. "When we were on the bench last night talking to her, I got a sense of fatalism from her, like she had somehow been waiting for this her whole life."

Spooky scooted closer to him; she needed the contact as much as he did, but that was as far as she was going to go until they got back to her house. They had decided against going away to a hotel for their honeymoon. Most of the hotels in Vegas were also casinos and Spooky didn't want to be anywhere near one of those.

She said, "I only got a glimpse of her memories second-hand. You know more about her than I do. Can you think of anything in her past that would lead up to this?"

"No, I don't remember anything significant. Her memories are fading much faster than yours have. I guess it's because I am not in contact with her on a regular basis."

"Which is fine by me!" she said, putting her arm through his and hugging it tightly to her side.

"You're not still jealous?" he teased, kissing her on the nose as they turned onto her street.

"If I ever have to connect that deeply with another man, you'll be singing a different tune," she muttered, looking up at him with a wry expression.

His left eyebrow lifted. "Oh? And why would you ever have to connect with another man?"

Spooky giggled. "You never know what the future might hold," she said as the limo stopped in her driveway. She and Balcher waited impatiently for the driver to come let them out. They were advised by Zack that it was proper limousine etiquette and they promised to behave no matter how much of a hurry they might be in to get the honeymoon started.

Balcher got out of the limo and then turned to help Spooky out, except that he didn't let Spooky's lacy high-heeled shoes touch the ground. He lifted her into his arms and carried her up onto the porch and, holding her up with one arm, he retrieved the key to the house from his pant's pocket and then opened the door before carrying her over the threshold.

They entered the house to find tables in both the kitchen and the living room laden with all kinds of food and cake and other delicacies, as well as any other amenities associated with a wedding reception, but with one glaring omission. Wedding guests. They had it all to themselves.

"Wow! That's a lot of food!" Balcher murmured in amazement as he kicked the door shut behind him.

"Don't worry," Spooky said, "you're gonna need every bit of this food and more over the next couple of days."

Balcher laughed aloud. "I am, huh?" He kissed her soundly, holding her against him as her legs slid to the ground so that she could stand on her own two feet.

She pulled away from him breathlessly, desire strong in her eyes. Then a twinkle appeared in them and she laughed as she pushed him away. "Dibs on the cake!" she yelled, running to the table to grab a slice of the mega-rich dessert with her fingers and smashing half of it into her mouth.

Balcher was right behind her. "Only if you're sharing," he growled, catching her up for another kiss, this one tasting of frosting. He couldn't believe that when given the choice of honeymoon sex with him and wedding cake, that Spooky chose the cake.

Well, actually, he could.

He laughed again and plunged whole-heartedly into the spirit of things, sampling the whole array of the wondrous food.

Of course, they saved the best for last.

Each other!

Epilogue

"I'm still not sure I like this," Spooky said grumpily as she wiped the sweat from her eyes with the hem of her sweatshirt.

"Come on, sweetheart, just ten more minutes and we can go for Chinese takeout," Balcher said, grinning.

"It's not fair. You're so much bigger than me."

"Think of it this way. If you can take me down, you can take anybody down."

"But we've been doing this for months now, and I haven't taken you down even once!" she complained.

"You will. Let's try it one more time." Balcher came up and grabbed her from behind with his muscular arm stretched around her throat.

Spooky didn't give him a second to get ready for her. She struck him in the ribs with her elbow and then she grasped his arm and twisted it around the way he showed her. To her amazement, it worked. She had his elbow in one hand and his thumb gripped in her other hand, and she twisted it back until he went down onto his knees.

"Enough!" Balcher yelled.

Spooky heard clapping and she grinned at Renda who was watching the bout from the sidelines. Then she released Balcher's thumb. "I did it!" she said, dancing the dance of the triumphant.

"I told you that you could," Balcher said with a grimace. He shook his hand to rid himself of the pain she'd inflicted. Then he scrambled up to his feet.

Spooky grabbed his wrist and brought his thumb up to her lips. "Let me kiss it better," she said, winking at him.

We have company. You'd better watch what you're kissing better.

"I can hear you, Balcher," Renda said, shaking her head bemusedly. She had been taking karate and hand-to-hand combat lessons with Spooky and Balcher for the last two months at Spooky's request. When Spooky found out about Renda's abusive ex-husband, she took the woman under her wing, putting aside any jealousy she'd felt about the connection between her and Balcher

"Oops, I forgot," he said, throwing Renda a grin over his shoulder. "You want to grab some Chinese with us?"

She shook her head as she followed them out of their basement where all the exercise equipment was set up. Balcher was keeping his word about making Spooky work out on a regular basis and the workouts appeared to be helping her deal with the consequences of her clairvoyant visions as well. She was keeping her weight at a regular one hundred and twenty-five pounds. "Not tonight. I have to get back to the clinic. Thanks for the word you put in for me. I'm really happy for the first time in a long time."

"Are you still seeing auras?" Spooky asked as they reached the top of the stairs and came out into the kitchen. She motioned for Renda to follow her to the refrigerator for some orange juice. Balcher had just put them both through a pretty heavy workout and the drink was much needed.

"Yes. It's taken me a while, but I'm finally beginning to figure out which colors mean what. The variations are pretty wide. For instance, purples and pinks usually mean passion or love. You two practically glow with those colors."

Spooky literally turned pink at that, but Balcher just grinned.

Renda continued, "Blues have several meanings, depending on their hue. But there is actually a blue that I think represents depression. Can you believe it? People can really be blue. It makes you wonder about the affect of auras on our language, doesn't it?"

"Not really," Spooky said, sitting down at the kitchen table. "I've never seen auras myself, but they're mentioned a lot in the books I have on the paranormal. I imagine that seeing auras is pretty commonplace among psychics."

Renda nodded. "I saw a pregnant woman the other day and it was the first time I saw a particular shade of green. The aura was surrounding her belly and I thought it meant new life or earth mother, but it turns out it was a case of pre-clampsia."

"You're kidding?" Balcher asked, taking a glass of juice from Spooky, but looking at Renda in amazement.

She smiled. "Nope. I've seen cancer, too. It's a dirty greenish-yellow color."

"How do you know that for sure?" Spooky asked.

Renda shrugged. "It's just a case of matching a known diagnosis with the aura's placement and color. Most illnesses come across to me as greens and yellows or a mixture of the two. I'm really excited by this. If I can quantify each illness and match it to a certain color, can you imagine what a diagnostic tool that would be?"

"It sounds amazing, that's for sure," Spooky said. "I'm curious, though. Have you attempted to heal anyone else, yet?" The 'else' Spooky was referring to, was when Renda healed Spooky's broken finger after a karate accident last month. The connection formed during the healing also brought Renda and Spooky closer together, making it easier for Renda to accept the warm friendship that Balcher and Spooky were offering to her.

Renda shook her head. "I remember what you told me, that there are consequences to connecting with anyone that deeply. I know that it should only be done as a last resort. So, don't worry. I haven't come across anyone with symptoms that were that urgent yet."

"What about your clairvoyance?" Spooky asked.

"It's still there, stronger than ever. You know, if I was not afraid that Alex would find me, I could probably be working at the most prestigious diagnostic hospital in the country by now. The clairvoyance would help me to get the most complete patient history imaginable, and the auras would let me know what was wrong with the patient before the first test was even scheduled. I'd be the superwoman of the medical world."

Spooky frowned at the mention of Renda's husband. "What's new with Alex Hamilton? Are you still having the dreams?"

"Yes. It's almost like my mind runs out into the cosmos during sleep and checks on his location. I think that I'll know it when he comes for me the next time."

Balcher put his two cents in. "I can do you one better than that, Renda. I can put the fear of God into that worthless bastard and make sure he never comes after you again."

Renda shook her head. "You and Spooky have done enough for me. You kept my true name out of that Brandson episode. Alex would have found me in a heartbeat if you hadn't. He's so rich, he has several law enforcement officials in New York on his payroll and they would have told him if my name came across any law enforcement databases. Don't worry! I haven't felt this safe in years. I truly believe that I have an edge against him now. I don't want to stir things up unless I have to."

"It's a shame that you can't practice medicine under the name Graycloud," Balcher said. "The world lost a really great doctor when you were forced to give up your practice and go on the run."

"Alex knows that Graycloud was my grandfather's name, so he'd be checking that alias as often as he checks my married name, Hamilton, and my maiden name, Garrett. But don't worry, you've given so much back to me getting me this job at the clinic. I feel useful again for the first time in a long time. I'll be all right." Renda finished her juice and put the glass in the sink and then she headed for the door. "I really need to be going, now."

"Well, you know where we are if you need us," Balcher said, getting up from the table and walking Renda to the front door. Spooky came up beside him and they waved to her as she drove out of their driveway.

"She's going to be all right," Spooky assured him. "That clinic was just the medicine she needed."

"I told you about that, didn't I?" he asked. "I was riding by the place and it just started glowing. I stopped in and for a moment couldn't figure out why I was supposed to be there. Then I saw the sign advertising for an assistant and Renda just popped into my mind."

"You told me," Spooky said in bemusement. Balcher was still so new to all of this stuff that he couldn't help recounting the amazing occurrences that happened to him. Saying them aloud made them feel more real and assured him that he wasn't crazy. She knew the feeling.

Maybe that's why it felt so good to keep Renda close by. Renda understood what they lived with because she was part of it now. It was almost like they'd formed a secret society.

They were all safe for now. Alexander Hamilton didn't know where to find his illusive wife, Renda, and so far as she and Balcher knew, no governments were hot on their trail. When Balcher opened Brandson's safety deposit box, he found copies of the tapes Brandson had made from his phone's video. It was impossible to know if they were all there, more than likely they weren't, but Brandson kept no diary or record of his investigation of Spooky. That made them both breathe a little easier. If he'd kept a diary, then he would have placed a copy in the box. Besides, knowing of Balcher's ability to go outside of Real Time, especially when combined with her ability to teleport, Spooky was sure that they could handle anything that might be ahead of them.

Spooky shut the front door and leaned into Balcher for a lingering kiss and then a hug. "We need a shower before we go out for Chinese," she said, loving the way his heart sounded in her ear as she leaned against his chest.

Waves of comfort and warmth poured into her as she held him, the feeling just as amazing as the first time she experienced it.

Meant to be...

The whisper echoed in her head and she smiled.

Meant to be...

Spooky squeezed the love of her life and then gave him a pat on the behind. "Hurry! I'm starving!"

"Me, too! Last one to the shower is a rotten egg!" Balcher said taking off for the bathroom. They raced to the shower amidst giggles and it was a long, *long* time before they actually made it to the Chinese restaurant.

About the Author

Tanis Rush has a degree in Commercial Art from Jacksonville State University of Alabama and has worked as a billboard artist, a technical graphic artist and has designed signs—neon and otherwise—in a nearby locality. However, she found that writing was what she loved most to do. As author of *Deadly Masquerade* and *A Dangerous Game*, it is obvious that her interest lies in romance novels loaded with suspense. But in her latest novel, her interest in the paranormal came to the forefront. She lives in a small town in Northwest Georgia with her family.

Made in the USA
Charleston, SC
17 April 2014